Samuel Williams Cooper

Think and thank : a Tale

Samuel Williams Cooper

Think and thank : a Tale

ISBN/EAN: 9783337024253

Printed in Europe, USA, Canada, Australia, Japan

Cover: Foto ©Andreas Hilbeck / pixelio.de

More available books at **www.hansebooks.com**

THINK AND THANK

A TALE

BY

SAMUEL W. COOPER.

ISRAEL'S MISSION
IS PEACE

Philadelphia:

THE JEWISH PUBLICATION SOCIETY OF AMERICA.

1890.

TABLE OF CONTENTS.

CHAPTER IX.

CHAPTER X.

CHAPTER XI.

CHAPTER XII.

CHAPTER XIII.

THINK AND THANK.

CHAPTER I.

A BROTHER IN NEED.

"Give it to the Jew!"

A fair-haired lad stood confronted by a score or more excited boys, who jeered and tormented him with that persistent brutality which comes of persecution. He was not "one of them," else surely he would have found some defender against their unfair attacks.

His only advantage lay in the fact that his back was to the wall; but with so many enemies, this proved only a small protection. Some of them made passes with their fists, as if to strike him in the face and body; others pinched him or threw dirt and balls of paper at him, and all, in turn, taunted him, and the end of their cries was the same:

"Give it to the Jew!"

The afternoon sun shone full upon the boy as

1

he stood there bravely; there was nothing to show his fears, save a nervous twitching of the lips and eyes. Poor little chap! He was not more than ten years old, and his weakness should have proved a sure defence. But his name had been enough, and the other scholars had soon begun towards him, in their way, the same kind of persecution that their fathers had practised toward his people for so many centuries.

"How is young Father Abraham, to-day?" cried a burly, shock-haired fellow, who seemed to be the leader of the boys. "Where are Moses and Isaac and Jacob and the others of your great tribe?" "Where are your asses upon a thousand hills?" "Where is your big brother?"

"If he was here, George Owen, you would none of you dare treat me so," the little fellow answered, his voice trembling with emotion. "Because I'm a Jew, it's no reason for you all to get at me at once."

"Come on, Mr. Isaacs," Owen scoffed and squared off at him as for a battle, and then suddenly slapped him in the face with his hand.

Abraham swung the books, at the end of his strap, over his head, and the boys who were near, including Owen, sprang back in fear; but not for long, and they once more gathered about, like flies, annoying him in all the small ways they could think of.

Again and again he beat them off, only to have them return with laughter and mockery. He was sore at heart and bitter tears came to his eyes, but he would not beg them to have pity on him; the spirit of his race was with him, and he bravely kept up the battle. At last, while a number attacked him on one side, Owen, on the other, seized the books and tore them away, leaving Abraham almost defenceless.

" You're cowards," the boy cried. " And you don't dare fight me single-handed; I'll fight you all, one by one."

" You will, will you?" Owen said. "Stand back, boys, and let me have a crack at the beggar of a Jew. I'll show him something."

As they drew away, he aimed a blow at Abraham which, had it taken effect, would, beyond doubt, have knocked him down; but the boy was too quick and sprang aside—his adversary running into the wall with the force of his assault. He turned, the sun was in his eyes, and Abraham struck him full upon the side of his head with his fist—a blow that staggered him, though the hand that gave it was weak and unused to fighting.

Some one in the crowd was fair enough to cry, " Well done, Jew !" and the bully, blind with mortification and rage that a boy half his size should have met him so, rushed again, wildly, at his opponent, and the two clinched. They struggled for a few moments, until the weight of Owen was too much for Abraham, and he fell heavily beneath his foe, who, disregarding all the laws of school warfare, struck him with his fist in the face.

How long the others would have allowed such brutality, was not to be known, for, before many blows had fallen, some one cried : " Here comes Moses," and a boy ran across the school-yard, and flinging aside those who stood in his way, took the bully by the neck and dashed him violently to the earth.

Abraham was uninjured, save for a bruise or two. Moses helped him to his feet, then turned and looked calmly at the crowd that now stood silent before the tall muscular figure and the bravery of the boy.

" You are a set of low, miserable curs, to treat a little fellow so," he said, deliberately.

"YOU ARE A SET OF LOW, MISERABLE CURS, TO TREAT A LITTLE FELLOW SO."

He spoke no other words to them, but there was passion in the voice; the clear eyes flashed; and about the mouth was a set look of fearless strength that caused them to fall back, quietly, as he passed across the yard with his brother.

" You had better let Moses alone, Owen," said Noel Hilton, the boy who had called out the cheering words to Abraham during the fight. " Look, he is all bone and muscle!" pointing to the retreating figure, as Owen arose. " You can lick his little brother, after he is tired out, but Moses is nearly as large as you, and I fancy he will be boss of the school, now, if you don't take care."

Noel Hilton was a boy of great wealth and likely to come into a title in later life. He was a fop in his dress—constantly appearing with some new and fanciful article of attire, yet a well-knit, manly chap, withal, who, while he seldom quarrelled with his school-fellows, managed, in some way, to maintain his independence, never hesitating to speak his mind and stick up to it, too, on all subjects which interested him.

Perhaps custom had rendered him privileged, for Owen made no quarrel with him, and said, sullenly, by way of answer:

" We'll see about that."

CHAPTER II.

TROUBLES AT SCHOOL.

Moses Montefiore and his brother had been at this school less than two months.   It was called St. Denis, and situated in Kennington, a part of the City of London.   The boys knew the school as "Denis," without any prefix; most of them found that there was very little of the saint about the place.   Moses and his brother were day-scholars; that is, they lived at home, and attended only during study hours.   Many of the scholars lived at the school, while others boarded at the houses near by.

Moses Mocatta, the uncle of the two boys, had prepared them at home for school life, and they also had attended a primary class before coming to St. Denis.   Moses was among the first boys in the fifth form; Abraham, some few years younger, was in the third.   In their studies they did well; two healthy, manly lads, anxious each to do his part at school and be good friends with the other boys.

Yet their lives were made troubled and unhappy by distrust and dislike.

This was a hundred years ago, and the Jews, throughout England, as elsewhere, were the subject often of open persecution; at all times they were held up to the scorn and derision of those who called themselves Christians. Under the law they could not hold land, or have any place in the Army, or in the Government; and there were special fines and penalties laid upon them if they engaged in certain kinds of business.

Thus it was that the English boys took up the cry of the older people, and had delight in annoying their Jewish school-mates.

So far, by quiet manners and care, they had avoided any general outbreak with the others; but had been compelled to endure much.

Moses was a sturdy, determined lad, able to defend himself, but his fair-haired brother, whose sweet face and almost girlish ways made him an easy subject to tease, was constantly in trouble and needed protection.

Between the day scholars and the boarders a rivalry existed, which, as time went on, grew fiercer. George Owen was the ringleader among the latter, and never lost an opportunity of annoying his enemies; indeed, even the smaller boys of his own party were made miserable by his tortures. He had an able assistant in one of about his own age—Richard Doughty—generally known as Dick Dough.

As Moses was about leaving the school-yard, a day or two after their studies had begun, he heard cries of pain coming from a group of small boys, among whom he saw this fellow.

He hurried forward to find out what was the matter.

"Dick Dough is twistin' Joe's thumb, 'cause he won't be his fag," one of the small boys told him.

Moses looked over the heads of the surrounding crowd and saw a little fellow lying on the ground, moaning and crying, while his tormentor bent over him and twisted a cord about his thumb, until it almost cut through the flesh.

"I am a day-scholar, and I don't have to fag for you," he cried. "Get one of the boarders!"

Moses pushed the boys in front of him aside, and said:

"That's the rule here. Why don't you let him alone. You have no right to torture him so."

A face, red with anger, glared up at him.

"I'll give you a taste of it next, you Jew brat,"

and Dick, in his passion, gave the cord an extra twist.

"You boys are all home boarders," Moses said; "help me."

Dick, thinking a united attack was to be made on him, jumped to his feet, furious with rage, and made a wild rush at Moses; Joe, in the meantime, escaping.

Montefiore dodged the angry blows aimed at him, but it would have gone hard with him, had not one of the monitors come up at the moment.

"What's this row here, Dick Dough?" he said. "You are always fighting."

"It's the Jew, who interfered when I was playing leap-frog with the other boys."

The monitor looked critically at Moses.

"They oughn't to let such people come here," he said. "But we can't have any fighting. If the Jew annoys you again report it to me."

"He was twisting a small boy's thumb off with a cord and twister," Moses said.

"None of your tale-telling here," the monitor scowled.

Even the little fellows, who had been looking on with interest, did not seem to mind the injustice of the thing and paid no attention to Moses

as he left the yard.   He was a Jew, and they did
not care for him.

But, the next day, the boy felt happy when
Noel Hilton, one of the most popular among the
day-scholars, said to him:

"I saw that rumpus, yesterday, out of one of
the windows.   I want to tell you, I'm with you.
Dick's a brute.   You can count on me to back
you up now.   The boarders have no right to use
the day boys for fags, and this plaguing the little
fellows is mean work, anyhow."

After this, in his indifferent way, Noel was
always Moses' friend, and took his part whenever
there was a chance.

About this time Isaac Goldsmid, Moses' chum,
came to the school.   He was a quiet, even-
tempered fellow, but very determined; and,
together, the boys grew to be feared.   They were
seldom apart, and Isaac soon took his place with
Moses in the fifth form.   This companionship
and the careless friendship of Noel Hilton were
the only reliefs of school life.

With George Owen and Richard Doughty as
leaders, the scholars of all classes took up the cry
against the Jews, and no one lost a chance of tor-
turing them in all the little ways of school boys.

It was not that they had any true reason; not that the Jews troubled them; nor were the ring-leaders in the attack such very bad boys; but when once the cry of persecution was begun, it grew as days went by, and boys took part in it, who would have been ashamed to do other less dishonorable acts. To annoy the Jews was surely not wrong, for their fathers laughed when they were told about it, and even the teachers always sided with the other scholars.

The three boys were thus cut off from the rest by an invisible barrier, raised by older hands. Full of life and spirits and boyish fun, they were left out of all the amusements and sports.

It was a hard and bitter life. Boys love companionship; and the cruelty of losing all its pleasures and being set apart to be tortured, rendered the days at the school miserable, and made Moses rebellious and sick at heart.

CHAPTER III.

A TALK WITH UNCLE MOSES.

" Uncle, why do the other boys hate us so?"

Moses Montefiore was talking with his uncle, Moses Mocatta, of the troubles at the school, and asked the question, not that the thought was new, but because it was a subject always forced upon him.

His uncle had answered the query many times before. He was never tired of telling his nephew about his race, while he watched the brave boyish eyes, that seemed to drink in and treasure every word that he spoke.

After synagogue, on Friday evenings, when the children were blessed, while Moses sat at his mother's knees, Uncle Mocatta had begun his lessons; not that they seemed lessons, for he had woven into pleasant stories the legends of his people and their leaders. Afterwards, when the boy came to think, and questioned, he taught him the love of mankind, told of his race and their sorrows and persecutions; of their faith—unchanged in all the centuries that had passed, and of the day when they should return to their own land of promise—flowery and fertile as in days gone by.

So, when his pupil was confirmed and read his lesson aloud from the Book of the Law, there was a depth and power in his ways that made the Rabbi notice him as he had never noted others.

And his mother, Rachel, how proud she was

of her first-born ; yet, sometimes, when she saw the gravity of the boy, she was fearful, lest her son grow old beyond his years, and from over-thoughtfulness on one subject see but one side of life.

Then Uncle Josh, who had left his law office to go with a party of colonists to Africa, had come home, filled with marvellous tales of storms at sea, of pirates, of insurgents in the ranks of his party, of attacks by Indians, of the dusky kings and strange kingdoms of far-away lands, where there were fierce and curious beasts and birds of gay plumage—stories of all things that boys love to hear about. And Moses never grew tired of them—it mattered not how often they were repeated. He dreamed of strange adventures, and thought he was a soldier, like his uncle, leading his troops into the fiercest battles. The king, feeling that this roving life had unfitted Joshua Montefiore for his old work, in apprecia-tion of his bravery, had offered him knighthood, which he declined. He asked, instead, a commis-sion in the regular army. The request was granted, and he, first of his race, was regularly enrolled in the king's forces.

Now, Moses wanted to become a warrior, too,

and fight the battles of his king; and he was filled with the glory of England, and knew in his heart the bravery of her people and wished to be a free man among them.

And the battle had begun, not with the enemies of his king and country, but with the very soldiers whose banner he wished to lead to victory. So it was that he came to his uncle, once more, with the words that had become a cry of the heart, rather than a question:

" Why do the other boys hate us so?"

Knowing the trouble of the lad's heart, Uncle Joshua made no attempt to answer him directly.

"Moses," he said, "you say you wish to be a soldier. I want you to be one—not with a red coat and white cockade, but a leader in a good cause, where there is always fighting to be done."

" What is it, uncle?"

" I will tell you, some day, but now I want you to know that to be a soldier, either of your kind or of mine, you must first conquer yourself; after that you must conquer your friends, then your fellows, and, finally, the enemies of your people."

"Where does George Owen come in? Shall I fight him first?"

"Not if you can avoid it; but if you are

forced to defend yourself, I hope you will beat him so badly that it will be the only battle of that kind you will ever have to fight. Remember, patience and forbearance before the contest will make you doubly strong should the fight come."

"Uncle, the whole school is against us. I think I have a fair chance for first place in the form this term; but the boys jeer me and seldom talk to me. The best I can hope for is to be left alone. I feel like leaving, and getting rid of the whole thing. Other boys have hard enough times with their enemies, but I tell you, with the whole school against you, it is too much for any one fellow."

"It would be cowardly to leave; you won't do that?"

"No, I suppose not; but I should like to, sometimes"—thoughtfully.

"Conquer them, instead; by brains, by force of will, by calm persistency; if necessary, by your animal strength; more than all, by teaching them to know you as one fearless and determined in your faith and manhood—but conquer them. When they are yours, then come and talk to me about being a soldier."

Truly, it was no easy task that his uncle had set him.

Mr. Sever, the Head Master, wished to be just, but was unconsciously infected with the prevailing feeling against the Jews, although he seldom found anything in the conduct of either Moses or his brother of which to complain; the tasks that were set them were never slighted. The monitors, however, were tyrannical and unjust. They made it a matter of course to believe all tales and complaints against the oppressed ones, and to disregard their word.

George Owen, after his quarrel, doubled his hate, and lost no opportunity of persecuting his enemies, and stirring up the others to plague them with all manner of annoyances.

They called rhymes at the boys; spit-balls would strike them unawares; and, when Moses was absent, his brother was pinched and hustled about the yard with a cruelty that was never-ceasing. If any complaint was made by the teachers as to broken desks, or marked books, or bent pins placed upon chairs, or noises in the class-rooms, Moses or Abraham Montefiore or Isaac Goldsmid were almost certain to be blamed for the offence. But hardest of all to bear were the contemptuous words, and to have always the cold shoulder turned by those who had no cause whatever.

As the days went by, and Owen found that Moses avoided him, he grew more and more offensive; finally he, in his anxiety for revenge, devised a plan to bring his enemy into disgrace before both masters and scholars.

CHAPTER IV.

GEORGE OWEN'S REVENGE.

"By whom was this mouse brought here?"

It was Professor Heath who spoke.

During class hour, William Day, who sat next to Moses, had let loose a white mouse, that he had been keeping in his desk as a pet.

The little animal ran swiftly up the aisle, towards the Professor, and when it had almost reached him, sat up and looked about gravely.

Always on the alert for fun, the boys had noticed the escape of William's pet, and watched it, with half hushed titters and great interest.

The Professor, busy looking up a reference, at first did not notice the trouble. But when the mouse sat up comically before him, as if for a lesson, the whole class burst into a roar of laughter.

2

Then the Professor looked up, saw the cause of the disorder, and asked the question.

"It came from under that desk," George Owen said, pointing towards Moses.

"Is that animal yours, sir?" asked Professor Heath.

"No, sir; it is not," Moses answered.

"You may do two hundred lines, and be confined two hours, after school."

For some unknown reason, Professor Heath had an especial aversion to Moses. He never lost a chance of inflicting punishment and presumed guilt upon the slightest suspicion.

"Henry Wingate and William Day, you may catch this poor creature and take it out. We will not go on until that is done. The other boys may keep their seats."

Then William Day, with the most innocent face in the world, with great ease, captured his own pet, and said he would keep it in his desk until school was over.

This is how it happened that Moses sat in the class-room that afternoon as evening came on. He had finished his task of two hundred lines, and was now only awaiting the expiration of the two hours' confinement. Every one else had left the room. The soft light of the setting sun crept through the windows of the old school, and made the boy feel lonely and deserted. Bitter thoughts were in his heart, that he should have marks made against the average of which his mother would have been so proud, and be compelled to suffer for what he had not done.

It was quite dark in the corner where he sat, but, in the half-light, he could see clearly over the whole school.

Presently, some one looked through the door. Moses saw that it was Arthur Snape, a first form boy, who was Owen's fag. He was a timid little fellow, and his constant ill-treatment by Owen had made him sneaky. Moses thought he appeared especially guilty now, for he crept down the row of desks, looking nervously about him until he reached that of George Owen. This he unlocked with a key he took from his pocket, and put in a book and a box about six inches square. He then locked the desk, and quickly left the room, not knowing that Moses was there.

The second hour of confinement was soon over, and Moses gathered up his books to go home. While he was at his desk, he was certain that he heard a sound like the gnawing of a mouse, coming from Owen's desk, which was across the aisle from his own.   He thought little of it at the time, however, as it was a very common thing for the boys to keep pets of various kinds in the school-room —despite the danger of punishment.

Next morning, Professor Heath was somewhat late, and strode nervously up the aisle.   He looked irritated, and was evidently in a bad humor.   There was a spirit of expectancy on the faces of several boys, that Moses did not notice.

The Professor laid his books down rather noisily, took a key from his pocket, and tried to unlock the desk.   Something was the matter. He fumbled with the lock, and cried angrily that some one had been meddling with it.

All was silence.

The Professor muttered to himself, and then, with a loud exclamation, forced up the lid.

As he did so, a large rat jumped out, almost in his face, and. with a shrill shriek, scampered over the floor.

The Professor dropped the lid with a crash and started back in astonishment, uttering a cry of mingled fright and rage.   He grew livid with anger.

The outburst of laughter by the scholars was checked, and died away in a murmur of fear as they saw the effect of the joke. But the worst was to come.

The Professor opened his desk once more. The boys could not see him as he gazed into its depths. When he closed the lid and looked over at them again, there was less of anger than of desperation on his face.

"Do any of the boys know what was done with the roll of manuscript, taken from this desk?"

There was no reply.

"Answer me, at once," he cried, growing angry again. "It was a life-work of mine. I can never replace it."

But the boys were too frightened to speak.

He searched under his desk, and on the floor under the seats near by. Suddenly he stood up with a book in his hand. It was a well-thumbed volume.

"Whose is this?" he thundered. "Who brings cribs into this school?"

Silence again. He turned over the leaves.

"Moses Montefiore, come here!"

Moses at once went up to the desk and stood firmly before him.

"Did you break open my desk?"

"No, sir; I did not," Moses said, quietly, but with a trembling voice. "I know nothing of it at all."

"Then, how is it that I find under my desk a crib with your initials in it?" and he held up the book, and pointed to some letters scrawled there.

"I do not know, sir," Moses said. But, in his heart, he thought of Arthur Snape, on the evening before, with the box and book; and then the sound from Owen's desk.

"Do you mean to tell me you do not know?" Professor Heath cried, growing more furious with each denial. "You were punished for having a mouse here, yesterday, and now, not content with breaking open my desk and putting a rat in it, you steal my manuscript, that is worth more to me than your whole life. Go to your seat, sir. I shall report you to the Head Master to be flogged before the whole school this afternoon."

Moses went back to his place, hot and defiant with the injustice put upon him, but knowing how serious the matter was.

To be flogged before the whole school by the Head Master was a punishment reserved only for a serious offence, and second only in disgrace to expulsion. The monitors and professors had power to punish by caning; but, so far, Moses had escaped this indignity. And now, to be flogged before the whole school for something that he had not done! What would his mother say? And Uncle Moses?

The hours wore slowly away. Moses could not study, and he missed in his recitations on the simplest things. It was not fear of physical pain that troubled him, he cared nothing for that; it was the disgrace.

His punishment was reserved for the end of the day, when all the classes were assembled together for the closing of school.

The Head Master, who was a narrow-faced, hard-looking man, heard the complaint and report of Professor Heath, and then called Moses before him.

The boy never forgot the scene. At the announcement of his name there was a murmur from the school, that, as he left his seat and strode towards the Master, died into silence.

As he passed the first form boys, Moses caught the eyes of Andrew Snape. There was a pitiful look in them of fear, of sorrow, of guilt; and Moses was certain that this boy, as Owen's fag, had done the thing that he was about to be punished for.

"What have you to say?"

It was Professor Sever's voice, in cold, severe tones, merciless, as of a mind made up.

"I did not have anything to do with breaking open the desk. I knew nothing about it, until the Professor came in this morning."

"Where did this book come from?"

"I do not know, sir."

"Why does it have your initials in it?"

"I do not know, sir; I never use a crib; I never saw it before. Any one who could write might put those letters there."

"Do you know who did this thing? or whose book this is?"

"I do not know, positively; but I think I could point out the boys who did it."

Moses cast his eyes over the school. George Owen refused to meet them, and looked down, while he picked nervously at his desk with a pencil.

"What a mean, cruel face," Moses thought. "He is always telling lies on me. What do I owe him that I should be disgraced like this for him?" and he thought of his mother, and knew how it would hurt her.

Then he turned to his judges. As he did so, his eyes again met those of Andrew Snape. The little fellow seemed fascinated by the scene, but his face bore in it the anguish of a condemned criminal. It seemed to Moses to be saying:

"Don't tell; please don't tell! I couldn't stand it."

"Well, give your information!" said Professor Sever.

"I am not certain. I could not tell on them, anyhow. I am not a tell-tale."

The Head Master addressed the school:

"Is there any boy here who can tell where this manuscript is that has been lost? It is a work of such value that no money could buy it. Does any one know anything of it?"

But the school was silent.

Professor Heath and the Head Master consulted together in low tones. Finally, the latter said to Moses:

"Take off your jacket."

It was quickly thrown off. Two of the monitors were called up to hold him.

"You needn't hold me," Moses said. "I will not move."

There was something so fearless about the boy

that his judges told the two assistants they might
stand back.

The boy set his teeth as the Master came forward and raised the pliable cane. He could never,
afterwards, forget it all. The faces of the scholars
—curious and gaping with the cruel interest of
school boys; the thoughts that surged in his brain;
the heated anger; the humiliation, then the hiss
of the stick as it descended and the vile pain of
the stroke. He knew not how many times it rose
and fell, but he was certain that he made no
outcry.

Flogging is brutal; it debases both master and
scholar. There is a devil in the hearts of most
men that arouses with the taste of cruelty, like a
beast of prey over blood. It makes them more
furious with their failure to evoke signs of pain.
Professor Sever was not different from other men
in this way. Moses was stubborn and would not
show his suffering by tears or cries, and so the
Head Master did not cease his brutality until his
arm was tired, and the back of his pupil covered
with great welts that burned like the tracks of a
red-hot iron.

" You may replace your jacket."

The boy was almost fainting with pain; but

he pulled himself together, by a great effort, and strode down the aisle to his place.

The other boys looked at him curiously. It had been their custom to cry as loud as they were able, and thus, by making the punishment seem severe, escape the worst. They had never seen a boy beaten as this one was, yet he uttered not a sound through it all—and they felt that here was a lad different from themselves, and something of the admiration for a hero came over them. For many a day, afterwards, they talked together of the nerve of the Jew.

But the agony of the physical pain was nothing to the mental torture of Moses. His mind was bitter; the world was all wrong to him, and he wished he might die for very shame; for, without wrong-doing on his part, he had been flogged by the Head Master before the whole school!

CHAPTER V.

A BULLY'S DOWNFALL.

In the indignation of her heart, at the story of her son's trouble, Rachel said that Moses should not return to the school.

"But, mother," he said, "I had rather go

back; I couldn't leave now; I didn't do it, and
time will show it so to everybody.   I will fight it
out, no matter what happens."

And his mother knew that it was for the best
that he should not give up.   The flogging of
scholars, in the days of which I write, was not
considered of very serious moment by parents,
even when it was done without much cause.   In
this case, however, it had hurt Rachel deeply to
hear of this injustice to her son.   She felt it to be
one of the petty race prejudices from which she
had so often suffered and which she knew so well
—the bitter of which was to be for always the
heritage of her son.

Moses had thrown himself down upon the rug
in front of the bright wood fire, and his head was
resting on his mother's knees.

So they sat in silence for many moments.
Was it wrong, she wondered, to love her boy so
dearly—to worship any one so, save God; to feel
in her heart such wild anger at those who injured
him.   The fire crackled merrily, and a warm glow
of light was about him.   After a time she laid
her hand on his head.

"I am glad you are going back, my darling,"
she said, softly.   "I am glad you are to be a

manly man. Keep on bravely; the sky will be brighter soon. You will be cleared of all this trouble, and will win the boys to your side in the end."

"With all my efforts I have only one friend, so far, except Isaac, and that is Noel Hilton. Isn't it strange, mother, that a boy who is such a swell and fop should be so independent in his likes?"

"He's not a bully; a swaggerer is not always a coward, Moses, and fashion in dress does not always change a boy's heart. To have Noel on your side is a good beginning. Keep on, dear boy, and the others will turn at last."

"That's what Uncle Moses says; but I have been trying so hard, and look what has been done to me!"

"I know; but you must not be out of heart. If there were no trouble, there would be no credit for fighting it."

"All boys have troubles, but not as many as we do. This is the sort we can't help. I try so hard to be kind, and because they can call me a Jew they hate me."

Rachel knew of the many trials there must be in all lives, no matter how free from care they seem, and her heart was full of sorrow and love for her brave boy. She leaned down and kissed his hair softly, and whispered to him words of comfort; and he felt at peace, and had new strength for the morrow's battle.

The next morning, Moses and Isaac Goldsmid set off for school together, Moses very stiff and sore in body, and his heart bitter and rebellious, yet quiet, with determination.

"Who did the trick?" Isaac asked.

"I am certain it was put up by Owen; and that poor little sneak, Snape, helped carry it out."

And Moses told all he had seen in the school room, the evening before the trouble.

"How did that crib, with your initials in it, get there?"

"That was part of the plan, no doubt. Owen wanted to get even with old Heath, and hurt me at the same time, and he put my initials in the crib, and purposely left it on the floor, or got Snape to do it."

"What was it the Professor lost?"

"Something about 'Oliver Cromwell,' I believe. He has been at it for years; looked up a lot of references and stuff. It's a big loss to him. I wish I could find it for him. It's no wonder the poor chap's mad."

"I think you will have to fight Owen before he'll learn to let you alone. If you can thrash him, and clear yourself of this bother with old Heath, things might come all easy."

"I believe I can lick him, if I have a fair chance. He's a miserable, sneaky scamp."

The class was unusually quiet on this day. The punishment of Moses had had a sobering effect on the boys. They looked at him curiously, and at recess several of them asked him how he felt. Noel, in particular, was very kind to him.

"I know you didn't put that joke up on old Heath," he said. "It was Owen who did it; it's because you thrashed him so that he's trying to hurt you this way. You'll have to lick him again, I fancy, before you'll get rid of him."

George Owen seemed in particularly good humor. He did not speak, but his laughter, as he passed with Dick Doughty, was evidently intended for the ears of his enemy.

How bitter Moses felt towards him, no one can know. There was something so contemptible about all that Owen had done, that he loathed him, rather than hated with the spirit of anger. To look upon this boy, who could drag a little fellow into his plans, deliberately conspire to put the blame for his own offence on another, and then jeer about it, made Moses sick with disgust.

"How is your Jew friend's back?" Owen said to Noel, later on.

"Like yours would be, if the guilty one had been flogged," Noel replied, sharply.

"Look out you don't get your own sore," Owen cried, angrily. But he went on without any attempt to fight about it.

The loss of his manuscript had made Professor Heath more nervous and irritable than ever; but Moses was unfailing in his studies and recitations, and life began to drift back into the old ways.

George Owen was not satisfied. The boys in his set taunted him sometimes, that he was afraid of the Jew in a fight, and Noel had annoyed him by telling him that if he did not look out Moses would beat the life out of him.

Several days had passed and it was a half holiday. A large number of the scholars gathered about the doors to talk over their plans for sport. A slight snow had fallen in the night, and some few snow balls were being thrown about.

· Moses and Isaac Goldsmid crossed the yard

together on their way home. Isaac stopped for a moment to talk with Hilton, and his companion lingered waiting for him. A number of snow balls fell about him, but they came from a distance and missed their mark.

Presently Owen, urged on by the taunts of his companions, made a hard ball of slush and mud and approached close to Moses, with the evident intention of throwing it at him.

"Don't throw that at me, or I'll hurt you," Moses said, fiercely.

Almost at the same instant he was struck with the missile on the side of the head, and the slush and mud spattered all over him.

An attack from such a source stung him to anger.

"You shall pay for this," he cried.

"A fight! a fight!" was heard from several boys, and in a moment a crowd surrounded the combatants.

There was nothing to be said between them. In an instant Moses threw off his coat, and Owen did likewise.

Goldsmid stood by his friend to see fair play, and Hilton backed him up.

Owen was championed by his lieutenant,

Richard Doughty; yet, though he was the bully of the school, the dislike to the Jews was so deep that he had the support of most of the larger fellows. The little boys, it is true, from the many cruelties put upon them by Owen, were in sympathy with Moses, though they dared not say so.

"I want you to know that I intend to see a fair fight, according to the rules," Hilton said, that every one might hear. "There has been enough meanness towards Monti in this school, and if you fellows are gentlemen, you will see this thing fought square."

"That's so—that's so—" came from a number of voices.

Fighting was not considered much of an offence at the school, provided it was fairly conducted. So much interest was taken in wrestling and boxing, and like sports, that an affair with fists was looked upon more in the light of a trial of strength than a serious matter. The monitors and teachers did not interfere unless it was absolutely necessary.

The two boys were not well matched in size. Owen was heavier and stronger. To the careless eye he was a certain victor in the coming contest.

But one used to measuring fighting values would
have seen in him many defects. He was clumsy;
his legs were not as well put together as his arms
and body, and, in a contest of endurance, his
powers were uncertain.

His antagonist, on the other hand, though
slight, was perfect in his physical development.
He had the clear health of his race. His straight,
muscular legs, the tense lower arms, displayed as
he rolled up his sleeves, and the general air of
compact strength marked him as one whom Owen
might well fear.

"Take time; play out his wind," Isaac said, as
his friend stepped out and threw up his fists.

Owen, though not a coward, would gladly
have avoided this fight. But he knew his place
in the estimation of his followers depended on
success; and their taunts and the excitement had
aroused him to wild anger.

He rushed furiously at Moses, who dodged
him. Again and again this happened.

"Hurrah! Hurrah for Owen! The Jew's
afraid," cried Doughty and two or three others.

"Hold your jaw," Noel said; "the fight has
not begun yet."

At last, as Moses sought to avoid his enemy

once more, his foot slipped and his opponent
struck him, as he fell, a hard blow on the side of
the face.

This success was greeted with applause by the
bully's followers.

"Keep it up," Isaac said, after Moses had
recovered. "You have winded him badly, now.
A little more, and then you can fight him to win.
Don't get rattled by anything. Science and pluck
will tell. Don't hurry."

The next round, and the next after that,
passed with a few blows upon the body of each;
much avoiding and parrying by Moses and wild
pursuit by Owen.

"Now," Isaac said to Moses, in low tones, "give
it to him! End him, once and for all. Your whole
future here depends on it. Don't fail."

It was a fight now; blows fell upon both, hard
and fast, and when a pause was called, neither
could be said to have the advantage, although
Owen was the most severely punished—his face
bore the marks of two or three straight-out hits.
His endurance was fast leaving him.

Again the boys met.

Owen tried to rush in upon his adversary and
blind him with the rapidity of his attack. He

aimed more than one foul blow, but Moses parried well, avoided his wild rushes, and when chance offered, struck him on the side of the head and knocked him down with the suddenness that told of a hit from the shoulder.

Owen did not rise for some seconds.

"Do you give up?" Isaac asked of Doughty.

"What do you take us for?" Dick answered. "We are just beginning."

"He's beaten; tell them we are satisfied," Moses said to Isaac.

"Remember all he has done to you; the flogging you got. This means your peace of life. You owe him nothing for lies and tattling. Give him enough this time. Show him who you are, and stop his bullying forever."

Owen stood up once more. His eyes were inflamed with anger, and the bruises on his face made him a very ugly-looking enemy. But his wind was gone, and he began to feel that defeat was on his track.

He could not get a blow on Moses' face, and struck him but twice lightly on his body. Once, twice, thrice he was struck himself—hard, honest blows, filled with some return for his misdeeds to Moses. Each time he grew weaker. He lost his head; he saw the disappointed faces of his followers, knew that the victory was leaving him, made one wild rush in his anger, and then received such a blow in the face that it was half a minute before he knew that he was lying flat in the mud, with Dick Doughty holding his head, and the crowd closed in about them.

The fight was over.

Owen's days of bullying were ended, so far as Moses was concerned. The Jew had beaten him by his science, pluck and endurance.

CHAPTER VI.

A MYSTERY CLEARED UP.

Do not look upon life as a fight, you who have read the preceding chapter. Rather think and know the world as a place where kindness and determination can do more than all else. Happiness cannot be found in crushing others, even though they are your enemies. To each one, I say, lend your efforts towards the time to come, when, as men, you will live with help in your hearts for each other, when life will be more to you than a struggle for wealth and selfish desires.

Then, if you are forced into a quarrel, you will be doubly strong. Fight fair, be open and win.

Moses had been patient, he had endured until his life became miserable, and when the time came, the battle was his and the bully of the school was conquered.

But his victory was more than that. It was not a mere brawl between two quarrelsome boys that he had taken part in. That one could so calmly bear the insults heaped upon him day by day; that he could take a flogging for another's ill-doing and not tell or cry out; that, when the battle was forced on him, he had displayed such calmness, such skill—and, above all, had beaten the braggart and bully who controlled the class—it was more than the downfall of Owen—it was a conquest of almost every boy in the school.

It was useless now for the defeated one or his second, Dick Doughty, and the few cronies they had, to try and stir up strife against the Jew boys. Victory was on their banners. It needed not Noel's help to show the truth; many of the others did not like those whom he defended, but they stopped their petty annoyances. Even the most brutal and careless had an involuntary respect for one who, in his boyish strength and bravery, could patiently endure so much.

And so, if life for Moses was not easy, it, day by day, grew less hard. He had hope now in his heart. He could see the effects of his efforts, and he planned to succeed, in time, in many ways.

For the masters were still against him. Professor Heath mourned, day and night, over his lost manuscript. It had been his pet; the years he had spent on it endeared it to him beyond any one thing else in the world. He had not the heart to begin the work anew.

Moses knew of this from the talk among the boys, and he could almost forgive the unjust flogging he had received when he thought of the sorrow of the loss, to one, the results of whose time and labor had vanished, by reason of the vicious spite of a school boy. He felt sure that if the manuscript had not been destroyed Andrew Snape knew where it was, and he determined to find out from him about the fact.

The little fellow was still in mortal fear of Owen. It was evident that his tormentor held over him the wrong he had done, and threatened to put all the blame on him, should he fail to do as ordered.

How to get the truth from him, and recover the lost manuscript was now the question with Moses. It must be done without letting the boy have time to see Owen, in case he confessed. If he did so, the manuscript, if in existence, would be hidden in another place or destroyed.

Montefiore kept a careful watch for his chance to speak to Andrew alone, but the boy avoided him; Owen, too, seemed always on the lookout lest he should peach.

At last, one day, Andrew was ordered to stay in two hours, after school, as a punishment for missing recitations. That afternoon Moses found that Owen was to play cricket on the grounds out of town; and he felt this was to be his looked-for opportunity.

As evening came on, he found Andrew alone in the school room. The boy was sitting at his desk, with his head in his hands, and did not notice Moses as he came up softly behind him. The poor little fellow was crying and in evident great distress.

"Andrew," Moses said, putting his hand on his shoulder.

The boy started up quickly.

"Let me alone," he said, trying to shake himself free.

"Snape, I want to talk with you," Moses went
on.

"What is it? I ain't done nothin' to you. I
don't know anything about it."

To Moses this was a confession of guilt.

"Andrew, I am sorry for you. I don't want to
hurt you. If I had, I would have told Professor
Heath that I saw you, the day before the trouble,
in the school room with a box with a rat in it,
and that crib."

"I didn't have nothing to do with it. It was
all George Owen. He did it."

"He made you do it, you mean. I know the
truth, and you had better tell me all about it."

"I didn't do it, I tell you. I don't know
nothin' at all about it."

"I will give you a chance, Andrew. If you
will tell me all, and give me the manuscript of
Professor Heath, I will not say a word about you
being in it, or Owen either. If you don't, I shall
tell the Head Master all I know to-morrow."

The mention of the Head Master was too
much for Snape. For days his nerves had been
overwrought with the wrong he had done, and

the weight of the lost manuscript on his mind; now he broke down completely.

"Oh! don't tell on me; don't tell. It was all George Owen. I didn't mean to do anything wrong. I will tell you everything. I can get the manuscript for you right off. Oh! don't tell; please don't tell on me."

It was just as Moses had suspected. The plot had been arranged by Owen, who had made his fag break open the desk with a chisel, put the rat in, and leave the crib with Moses' initials in it on the floor, and then bring away the manuscript that he knew the Professor prized so highly.

"Where is the manuscript, now?" Moses asked.

"It's in my box, up-stairs. I will get it right away, and I'll be glad when it is gone, too. Oh! don't tell on me; don't tell. I couldn't stand a flogging and all the fellows knowing."

"See that you don't say anything to Owen about this. I intend to give the writing back to the Professor to-morrow. If Owen threatens you, tell him you have told me all about it, and that, if he touches you, you will tell me, and I'll report the whole thing to the Head Master."

Andrew's time of punishment was up in a few

minutes, and Moses went with him and got the manuscript. The little boy was almost happy to get it out of his box, and seemed to be easier in his mind, now that Moses had taken up the task of returning it.

The next day, when Moses was called up for recitation, he carried the precious roll with him.

"Professor Heath," he said, as he held it out to him, "I have found your manuscript."

The Professor was so overjoyed at its recovery that he had no thought for anything else. He took the roll and examined it. It was uninjured.

"Where did you get this," he asked, finally.

"I got it, sir, by promising not to tell. I cannot break my word."

"Well, you have been punished for taking it, I shall not punish you for bringing it back. You may go to your seat. I am not convinced that I have not made a mistake about you."

At recess Moses found Owen alone, and spoke to him about the trouble.

"I want to tell you, now," he said, "that I have known that you did this from the beginning. I didn't want that poor little Snape to get punished, and so you have been saved. But if you ever bother that boy in the smallest way, or I catch you doing any mean tricks to any of the little chaps, the Head Master shall know all about it. You have been a mean enough sneak to me, but that doesn't so much matter. I want you to let the little fellows alone."

Owen mumbled something about not doing it, and then slunk away. He discharged Andrew as his fag the next day, and never spoke to him again, so fearful was he of trouble. The smaller boys generally did not suffer as much; and, in some mysterious way, it got to be a by-word with them when Owen did anything to them, to say: "I will go and tell Monti about it."

Little Snape had been ailing for some time and was out of sorts; now that the winter weather had set in he seemed worse, and, after a wetting from playing in the snow, had caught a violent cold that turned to fever. For many weeks he lay ill—too ill, indeed, to be removed from the school. His mother came down to stay with him, and, at last, nursed him back to convalescence.

One day, when all the school was ready for dismissal, the Head Master came forward and said:

"Moses Montefiore, come here."

Moses came up to the desk, frightened and fearing some new trouble.

The Head Master spoke to the school.

"Boys, I am a harsh man sometimes, but I try to be just. I want to make a correction and an apology for a mistake. This boy, Moses Montefiore, was flogged not long ago for breaking open the desk and stealing a manuscript of Professor Heath's. He was entirely innocent. He bore like a hero the flogging he got, rather than tell on a poor little fellow, who was led into doing the wrong by an older head. The little lad has been near to death, and has told us what he did; but asked that he be not required to tell the name of the real offender. If that boy is here now, he should hide his head for shame. He is a dishonored coward, and I can only hope that he will leave us or reform his ways. For Moses Montefiore I have nothing but the highest praise; and I ask his pardon before you all for my mistake. He found and returned the manuscript to Professor Heath, when, but for his efforts, it might have been lost for ever."

Professor Heath then came forward and took Moses by the hand and thanked him cordially, and asked his pardon for the injuries done.

PROFESSOR HEATH THEN CAME FORWARD.

There was a great murmur in the school, and Moses did not know what he said by way of answer, for his heart was too full of excitement and joy.

When he reached the school yard, there was a crowd of boys there, who, when they saw him, called out:

"Three cheers for Moses Montefiore!"

And all who were there joined in the cry of applause.

CHAPTER VII.

A STORY OF A LION HUNT.

" Uncle Josh has come!"

It was Moses' sister, Sarah, who opened the door, one day, and told him the welcome news.

Uncle Josh was a great favorite with his nephews and nieces. They would climb on his knees and search through his pockets, and always found sweetmeats or presents of some kind hidden there. Then, too, he was full of laughter, and had many wild tales of adventure about days spent in Africa.

To-night he had come in quite unexpectedly, home from his troops, on a short furlough.

When Moses entered the sitting-room, his uncle had drawn his chair before the blazing fire; the light shone on his brass buttons and red coat with dazzling effect and lit up his smiling face, tanned, like leather, by exposure to the sun and storm.

His nephew thought what a fine soldier he was—brave, hardy and frank.

"And how is my young captain?" his uncle cried, clasping his arms in his hands and holding him off that he might look well at him. "What a great boy you are growing to be. You will be as big as I am, soon; then you shall join the army, too, and come with me to fight the king's battles."

"No, no; don't tell him that," Rachel said. "He is my first-born. I could not let him leave me. Beside, I think it brutal, the way you kill people."

"But I am going, mother," Moses said, defiantly. "I won't work at anything else, I tell you that. You know I want to be a soldier, I always have."

"That is the way to talk," Uncle Josh said, laughing. "You will be a great fighter some day."

" I know Moses won't leave me, unless I wish it," his mother said, putting her hand lovingly on her son's head; he, for answer, caught and kissed it, and they went into supper, her arm about his neck.

" It is time for children to be in bed," Rachel said, an hour later, after the children had romped about the floor with the soldier and had climbed up on his knees to rest. But he put a great arm about each little girl and held them both close to his heart. Abraham sat on an arm of his chair, while Moses lay on the rug before the fire —sometimes gazing thoughtfully at the blazing logs, sometimes into the bronzed face of the warrior.

" We won't go until we've had a story," the two girls cried, nestling closer.

"What shall it be? A fairy story, or about the ocean, or about wild beasts, or what?"

" Tell us about the island and the savages where you went in the ship," Abraham said.

" What will you have, Moses," Uncle Josh asked, noticing that he said nothing.

" Well, I think about the lion hunt in Africa, when you got lost there in the wilderness."

" Yes, uncle, tell us about lions and tigers
4

and how they roar," Sarah said, lisping her
words so childishly that the hunter laughed
and roared like a lion so loudly that she was
afraid.

"All right, lions and tigers it shall be;
hold tight to me that they may not carry you
off."

The children huddled together closely. Their
father and mother sat at one side of the fireplace
and were happy in seeing the joy on the faces of
those so dear to them. There was no light save
that of the blazing logs heaped high in the
chimney, and ghostly shadows danced over the
walls of the room.

"When the colony on the island broke up, we
sailed for the coast of Africa, where all the people
are black, and it is so warm they only wear a bit
of rough cloth about them, instead of regular
clothing. Near to the coast we found a trading
post of just two or three huts, built of sticks about
as thick as my finger, stuck in the ground, with
the roofs of great leaves; and there was a fort,
with a high fence around it, made out of large
bamboo trees.

"The traders were Englishmen, who gave
cheap knives, beads and bits of cloth, and such

things, for ivory. With them they had a black man, who could understand both English and the gibberish.

"When we reached there, the traders were organizing a party to go up the great, broad river into the interior to get ivory, for they had heard of a king, far away, who had a hundred elephant tusks of great size and value. Jack Deane, Bill Hook, Tom Brady and myself, of our party, volunteered to go with them. We wanted to see the country, and the traders were glad enough to have us. There was danger in travelling; and with our muskets, pistols and cutlasses, we were a great addition to their forces.

"There were three boats—two large ones, made out of the trunks of trees, and a canoe, made of hides and bark, in which my men and I went by ourselves. We had a lug sail that we rigged, whenever the wind was favorable, and it saved us much hard work with the oars.

"You would have liked it, Moses. Monster alligators lay in the mud on the banks, or swam about like floating logs. We fired at them many times, but the bullets glanced off their thick hides.

"Once a huge fellow ran his back against our

boat, and almost upset it. He passed by, turned and was about to attack us again, when Tom placed his gun close to his eye and fired. There was a wild splashing of water, as the great tail lashed the waves, and our canoe rocked so that we had to hold on to the seats to avoid being thrown out. Then the smoke cleared away, and we saw the beast sink slowly out of sight. He was certainly dead.

" Beautiful cranes flew up from the high reeds, as we passed by; in the woods, along the shores, innumerable parrots chattered, and monkeys swung themselves down from limb to limb, to gaze gravely at the intruders. Once a drove of deer stood quite near in the water by the bank, and looked at us with such trusting eyes that I would not let my men shoot at them.

" At nights we encamped in such dry spots as we could find. We carried the three boats on shore, and made a sort of fortress or barricade. Outside of this we built a ring of fire, that the sentries kept blazing all night. We could hear the crashing of the undergrowth oftentimes, and howls of animals. Great eyes would be seen glaring out of the blackness, but they made no open attack on us; the fire kept them off.

"The stream gradually grew narrower, and the current was sometimes so swift that three men had to row to force the boat ahead. The banks, in places, were almost free from trees or bushes, and we could catch glimpses of plains and forests beyond.

"At last, our black guide told us that on the morrow we should certainly reach the land of King Teecoo, to which we were bound.

"The next day was long and hot, but towards sun-down we came in sight of a few huts on the shore; then men were seen waving their hands to us from a kind of wharf built out in the stream.

"Upon our arrival, after some talk between them and our interpreter, we were escorted to the king's palace, in the midst of a village. His hut was much larger than the others, and around it guards with long spears, stalked slowly and gravely up and down.

"This was a very savage tribe, and only the prospects of a great trade with the king could have induced us to take the risk of a visit. We had instructed the interpreter that he was to say nothing of our fire-arms. These savages did not know what they were, and we wanted to surprise them. There must have been a thousand of them about the building, and, as we stood at the palace door, they crowded around, and examined us and our belongings with great curiosity. Presently the king's head man came out, and seeing the crowd, flew into a violent passion, and poured forth a torrent of words. I don't know what he said to them, but they fled away in great haste.

"We were then led into a great empty-looking hall. The king sat on a platform, with a dozen guards about him. Our interpreter had a short consultation with him, the result of which was, that we were all put under guard, in a separate hut. Some fruit and raw meat were brought to us, and there we stayed until the following morning.

"We learned that King Teecoo had not said what would be done, nor made mention of our being put in prison; but there we were, and what to do we did not know. We held many consultations, but could not decide on any plan. It was useless to attempt to escape in the face of the difficulties about us.

"In the morning we were all again taken before King Teecoo.

"This time he was surrounded by hag-like

witches—old shrivelled women, with long finger
nails and white hair, in startling contrast to their
black faces, who crouched and moaned and mumbled wildly to themselves. Our interpreter was
called up before his High Mightiness.

"We watched the proceedings with great curiosity. We could not understand, even from the
actions, what was going on. The king talked,
the interpreter talked, and the witches kept up
their cries.

"At last the interpreter came among us again.

" 'The upshot of the whole matter is that there
is a large lion, that lurks somewhere on the outskirts of the village, that has killed a great many
of the king's subjects. This beast is such a scourge
that he is looked upon as a god, and when the
witches were consulted yesterday, as to what was
to be done with us, they decided that we must be
offered to the lion, one by one, as sacrifices, to
appease his wrath.'

"We had another consultation.

" ' Let's tell the king there is but one favor we
ask?' I said; 'that we be allowed to go into the
bush without being bound, and that our arms
shall not be taken away.' We called our guns
walking sticks.

"There was a grim kind of smile on his majesty's face as he granted the request. To-night, he said, the offerings must be begun, and we could decide among ourselves who should go first.

"This question we settled by putting as many grains of rice in a hat as there were white men in our party. One grain was colored red. The man drawing this was to go out that night and meet the lion.

" One, two, three, four, five grains were drawn, all white, and it was my turn. I put my hand in the hat, grasped a grain and drew it out.

" It was red.

"That night I was led forth to the outskirts of the town. Bill Hook had loaned me his two horse-pistols; I had two of my own and my musket, in addition. The natives pointed to a beaten track running into the jungle. It would have been death on their spears to have refused to go on, so I grasped my gun firmly and left them.

"Fortunately, it was a clear night, and the African moon, at its full, was overhead. No one can know the whiteness of that light—it was like a ball of silvery fire. The path was open, at first, but soon became overgrown and dense with under-

growth. I determined, as soon as I got out of
hearing of the blacks, to find a safe spot, near the
path, and wait for the lion to pass me. I, at last,
discovered a hillock, covered with long grass,
elevated two or three feet above the surrounding
land.

" On this I made my bed for the night.

" For a long time I kept a watchful eye on
every bush; my ears strained to catch a sound of
intrusion. There were noises of a thousand kinds,
near by and far away. I could hear the cry of
birds, flying over or chattering in the thicket;
African beetles droned about me and crickets
chirruped in the grass. A huge death-watch
ticked loudly at my feet.

" I was conscious, at last, that the heavy summer air and the fatigue that I had been under,
were making me drowsy.

" From my doze I was quickly awakened by
a crackling of the underbrush. I seized my
gun, which lay beside me, and looked in the
direction of the noise. Some huge beast was
coming up the pathway, as yet in dense shadow.
I could hear the sound of his breath and quick,
angry snorts.

" It was not until he was within a few feet of

me that he passed out of the bushes and into the open glade. The moon shone full upon him. He stood without motion, save the nervous lashing to and fro of his tail. There was a yellowish mass of mane and a body larger than I had ever dreamed of. He looked straight towards me. I was crouched in the midst of the reeds, where he must have scented me out.

"My hand shook as I lifted and cocked the gun. Should it miss fire, I felt certain I was a dead man. I raised the musket stealthily and aimed. The only visible target, now, was his head, and I felt that any ball would have glanced harmlessly from that skull. In one of my pistols was a great charge of slugs. At this short range I might blind him. I quietly drew the weapon from the holster. At this moment I saw the lion suddenly crouch, and, knowing he was about to spring, fired.

"There was a tearing and rending of the underbrush, mingled with cries and roars and mewing of the great cat in pain. Gradually all sounds ceased, and I felt that the danger had passed for the moment.

"Nervously and fearfully I awaited the dawn. At the first faint streak of light in the sky, I

"WHEN ALMOST AT MY FEET, I FIRED ONE OF THE PISTOLS FULL IN HIS FACE."

started down the path for the village. I had not gone far, when I heard a sound ahead of me. I stepped to one side and waited.

"There was a roar, then the crying of the lion, and I knew the beast was about to pass me again. He came creeping along the path from the village, stopping every now and then to put his paw up to one of his eyes, which I could see was entirely shot away. Nearer and nearer he came, until at last he saw me. The cry of rage, a mingling of a scream of anger and a roar, was awful. I raised my musket, although I determined not to fire until he was almost on me.

"Nearer he drew, stopping now and then to wipe with his soft paw the blood from his eye. This gave me a fair shot behind his foreshoulder. In my anxiety and haste I shot to the left and only broke his leg. He rushed at me on three legs, no longer able to spring. When almost at my feet, I fired one of the pistols full in his face. He rolled over, and after a few feeble struggles lay still.

"A party of the natives soon after came out to search for me, expecting to find only my bones. Together we made a litter of young saplings, and carried the huge animal to the village.

"When we were gathered before the king, he punched the lion with his fingers to see that he was quite dead, and asked how it had happened. They all pointed to me, and I stepped forward. We were outside the palace, in a sort of a public square. I determined to let the king see what a wonderful man I was. My musket was loaded with a charge of slugs, and flying towards us was a huge crane, very low down. He must have been six or seven feet across the wings, and offered an easy mark. When he got overhead, I raised my gun and fired. The bird fell at my feet. At the discharge, the king and his followers prostrated themselves, their faces to the ground, their arms spread out in front of them.

"'Tell him there is no danger,' I said to the interpreter. 'Say we only hurt our enemies, and that those who are our friends the fire-king protects.

"And so his majesty was conquered and treated us well, and we became great friends with the natives, and took away with us enough ivory to make our fortunes."

Esther lay fast asleep in the soldier's arms; Sarah blinked dreamily. After their mother had taken them off to bed, Moses' father and his Uncle Josh talked together for many hours, while he lay on the rug, and their words came to him drowsily, as from far away. He dreamed of strange adventures in strange lands, where there were black men, and yellow and red cranes, and he and Uncle Josh floated down a great river in a boat, and shot alligators. And then Moses, too, was fast asleep.

CHAPTER VIII.

THE SNOW-FIGHT AT KINGS COMMON.

Moses, Noel Hilton and Isaac Goldsmid were tramping home from school, one day in mid-winter. About noon the flakes had begun to drift slowly down, and, now, the snow was quite deep. It was growing colder and the wind blew sharply. The storm had set in for all night. Winter was in the air everywhere.

Of late, life at school had changed for the better for Moses and his friends. They were treated like the other boys, now, both by comrades and masters. They were taken into the sports, and Moses, from his strength and skill, gradually came to the front in the various games that were gotten up.   There was something about him that made him a leader among his fellows.

"To-morrow, we must have some fun, if this keeps up," he said, as they plowed through a drift at the corner of the street.   "We will have a battle with the town-boys out at Kings Common. If it only drifts deep enough to-night we will build a fort there."

"It is a half holiday, too," said Isaac.   "We can get a great crowd together and have a regular war."

"We will fix it up at recess to-morrow, and arrange the whole thing."

That night Moses got out an old book of his uncle's, on military tactics, and studied the best way of massing troops in victory and defeat. Isaac stayed with him all night.   At ten o'clock, when they went to bed, Moses scraped the frost off the window pane and looked out.

"Still snowing, like everything," he said; "it will be three feet deep to-morrow."

And such a storm as it was!   The next morning the oldest inhabitant looked out in wonder. Snow everywhere—drifted in some places above the windows of the first stories of the houses.   It was some time before the streets became passable.

The boys did not reach school until after the opening hour. The drifts were high and the walking difficult, but they plunged on, laughing, and threw handfuls of the snow at each other, and the way did not seem long. The clouds were breaking away. It was just cold enough to be inspiriting.

After the school had assembled, the Head Master called for attention.

"In view of the most unprecedented fall of snow to-day, we shall dismiss the school at noon, instead of one o'clock."

When the boys were free, what shouting there was, as they rushed into the yard. piled, in places, many feet high with snow.

Our three boys got some of the larger fellows together, and told them of their idea about the snow-fight. John Hornby, William Day, Robert Johnson, Joe Harris, Richard Doughty and George Owen were among the active ones. There were no longer any open hostilities between the latter two fellows and Moses and his friends. Owen was always a ready boy in any sport, and Moses and he were thrown together often. A crowd soon collected about them, and all wanted to talk at once, each with a different plan. The

uproar was great.   All were willing for the fight,
but they could not agree among themselves.

Moses got up on a box and spoke to them.   At
first they would not listen.

" Hold   your   noise," Noel   screamed.   " Let's
hear from one at a time.   Go on, Moses."

" My plan," Moses said, " is to go out to Kings
Common and build a big fort, make a lot of snow
balls, and then when the boys get out of the mill
they will give us a battle.   It will be a grand row;
much more fun than fighting among ourselves."

This plan was agreed to, by a unanimous vote.
The boys dispersed to get shovels and loose boards
with which to throw up their fortifications, and
boxes to make the snow into bricks.

When they reached the Common, which was
not far from the school, they found it was in
capital condition.   Against the high wall, at the
back, the snow had drifted, until it was quite covered ; while a large part of the ground in front
was swept bare by the high wind.   It only needed
their efforts for an hour or two to make the place
into a field of battle.

" Let's make a square fort."   " No, a round fort
is better."

There were many views.   Moses had drawn

his plan of the fortification on a sheet of paper. It was like this:

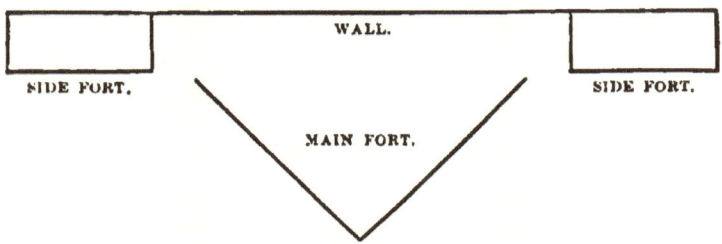

The boys crowded about him to see it.

"You see," Moses said, "a triangular fort like this is best, because the attacking party can't climb over the walls so easily; not able to get at them fairly. Then we can protect the whole range of walls easier in this shape, and we can have an entrance at either side, so we can sally out and pursue the enemy. These smaller forts, on each side, are the places where the sharp-shooters are placed to protect the entrances, and where the boys can stand who are to go out after the enemy to repulse them from the walls and take prisoners."

It seemed a good plan to the others, and was agreed on, at once, no one else having anything definite to offer. Moses had explained the whole idea to Noel and Isaac, and, together, they laid off the distances. There were so many boys, that

5

when they were all put at work, properly, they carried out the plans in a very short time.

The result gave them the wildest pleasure. It was better than they had expected. It was like a regular fort. The snow had been beaten into boxes about two feet square, and the blocks piled up on one another. This made a wall of snow that would resist a severe attack.

"We must have a supply of snow balls," Moses said; "four or five hundred will not be too many."

By four o'clock everything about the fort was in readiness for the attack.

All told, the school-boys numbered nearly fifty. Many of the smaller boys were ruled out as being below the age of recruits.

The army gathered within the walls of the fort.

"We must have a commander-in-chief," Noel said.

Then a wild discussion took place. There were various favorites. Finally, the choice of a leader fell on John Hornby. He was the largest and strongest boy at the school, and as he was preparing himself for the army, was supposed to have some knowledge of warfare. He was a manly, determined fellow; but lacked quickness and judgment. Noel, and one or two others, made a fight for Moses for the place, but it was without avail. The boys admitted that the fort was well planned, but they did not care for Moses to lead them. In deference to his followers, however, Hornby made him captain of one of the smaller forts.

In a short time the town-boys began to gather. They were led by a boy named Machin. Consultation was held between the leaders, and it was agreed that if twelve men of the attacking party got within the walls of the fort, the victory was to be considered won and hostilities were to cease for the time; the capturing party to hold the fort until it was retaken.

The armies were about equal in number, but the town-boys were larger and stronger and more reckless.

"They will beat us, if it comes down to a simple matter of brute strength. It will take science to hold this place against those fellows."

It was Isaac who spoke to Moses. He was his lieutenant in the side fort.

Presently his words were shown to be true. The engagement that followed was short and sharp. The town-boys made a united attack at one of the entrances. Hornby, supported by Doughty, Owen and Harris, fought manfully and hurled the invaders back, in a hand to hand conflict; but the enemy was too strong; the school-boys were beaten and the fort captured in a five minutes fight.

For that afternoon the sport was over. The town-boys were well pleased, and said they would be ready, the following afternoon, to defend their capture against all attacks.

At recess, the next day, a great discussion took place, as to who should lead the school forces in the attack on the fort that afternoon.

"Moses planned that fort, and it is a good one. I say we make him our captain this afternoon," Noel said.

Richard Doughty and George Owen were both anxious for the honor, but they were not popular with the others. After a fierce contest and debate, the question was put to a vote and Moses received a large majority.

He at once appointed Noel Hilton commander of the right wing, Isaac Goldsmid of the left, and John Hornby as his first officer, in the main body. Doughty and Owen were both given important places. They were good fighters, and Moses was too brave not to be honest.

A spy from the enemy's camp reported that they had soaked the walls of the fort with water, and it was now frozen hard. Also that they had made a large quantity of frozen ammunition. There was danger in the air.

At the second recess, the boys were all employed in soaking snow-balls and laying them out to freeze. They felt they must be prepared to meet the enemy on equal terms.

When school was dismissed there was wild excitement. All the school-bags and baskets were brought into use to carry the ammunition to the field of battle.

Moses carefully arranged the plans of campaign with his officers. He addressed the army and begged them to follow their leaders, not to fight wildly; and, above all, never to know when they were beaten. The honor of the whole school, he said, depended on their winning this battle. None of the frozen balls were to be used, unless the town-boys first began with that kind of ammunition.

The enemy soon assembled and occupied the fort in great numbers.

Moses was everywhere, among the attacking army, giving directions and showing the boys that it must be a matter of science if the fort was to be recovered.

Back of the wall, in front of which the fort was built, was a large factory yard. Moses had examined this, and found it quite free from snow. There was a shed built against the wall, on that side, and it was easy to climb up on it and look over into the fort. A tall, slow fellow, Roger Clerk, with four other boys, was detailed to lie in wait in this yard, and, when summoned, to climb on the shed and pour cold shot into the fort. All this was secretly arranged, Moses being the only one who knew of it, outside of those taking part.

A large beam of wood was secured, and three boys were appointed to use it as a battering ram on the main wall.

At last all was in readiness.

A red handkerchief was raised from the fort —the signal that the engagement was to begin.

The town-boys had received re-enforcements. The walls were black with them. It was a formidable task to attack them. Moses knew that unless skill was used they could never hope to regain the lost fort.

The invaders advanced in an unbroken line to the left of the fort. They were greeted with a volley of snow balls, even before they were fairly within range. But few were returned— only enough to make the appearance of a fight. Nearer and nearer they approached, while the firing was incessant. Then a retreat was sounded, and they withdrew out of reach. Again and again this was repeated. Three men of the attacking party were disabled, and a number wounded, but only enough to make them angry.

The third time they were withdrawn; there were loud complaints from several boys.

"Keep quiet," Noel said. "Don't you see we are playing them out of ammunition? When our time comes, we will have a big advantage, for they haven't much extra snow in the fort."

The battle now began in earnest.

The main army, led by Moses, made a united assault on the left entrance. Noel, with a detachment, was appointed to attack the side fort, in order to occupy the sharp-shooters and save their cross-fire on the others. Isaac was in charge of a corps, whose duty it was to cover the boys who worked the ram, from the fire from the main fort and the side fort on the right entrance. The ram

was to be used against the wall near the head of
the fort on the right.

With wild cries, the main body approached the
fort and strove for entrance on the left.   The air
was white with snow balls.   Again and again, the
boys tried to scale the walls, but they were ice—
no foothold could be gained.   At the entrance, a
strong body of troops beat off the invaders' fierce
attack, and captured two prisoners.   Noel, indeed,
with his corps gave the side fort all it could do to
avoid capture, and the main army was free to
attack without cross-fire.

The battle was fierce.   Neither side could gain
an advantage.   But the intrenchments the invaders had built so strong on the day before were
now the great obstacle against them.

Moses was in the midst of the fight.   One eye
was almost blinded by a ball that struck him, but
he encouraged the boys and cheered them on with
cries, in spite of the pain he suffered.   If the
victory was to depend on his attack at the left,
however, he felt they were beaten.   He wondered
what Isaac and the battering-ram were doing, and
whether it was time to summon his re-enforcements.   He had appointed a small boy as his aid,
to wait on the Common, where he could see the

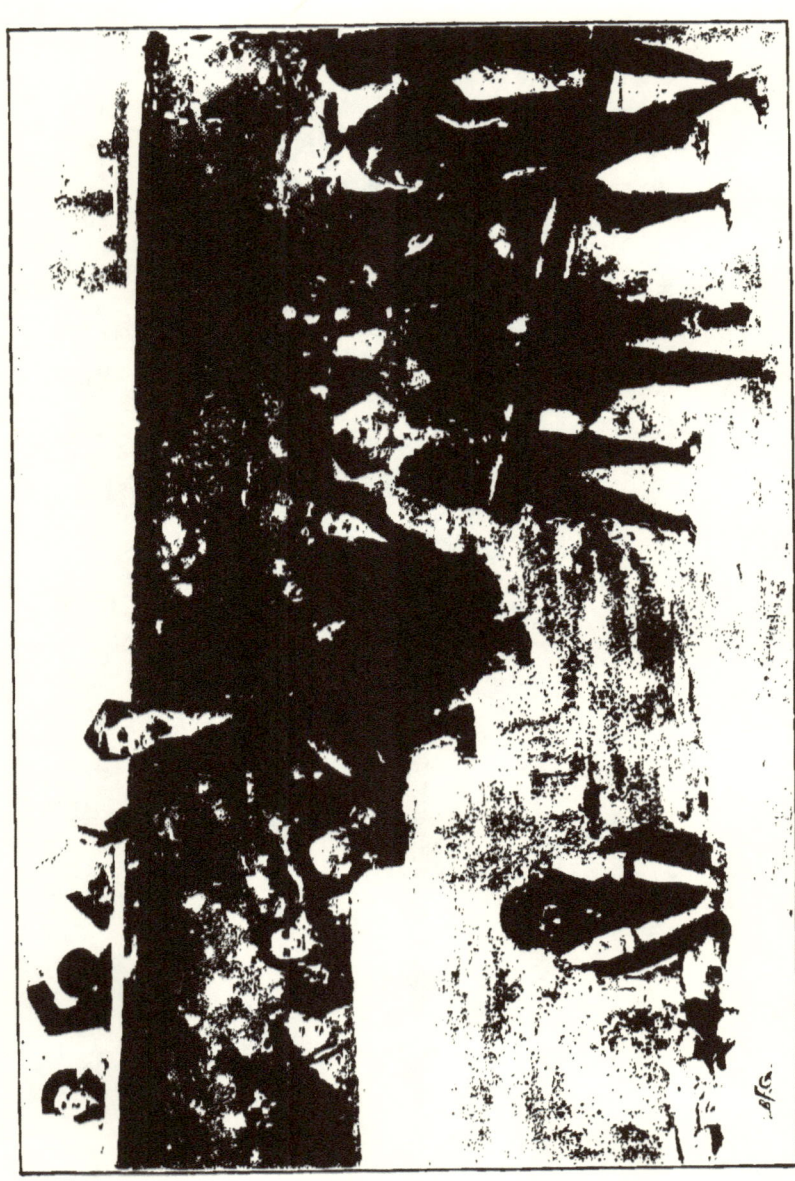

THREE STRONG BOYS, WITH A HUGE BEAM OF WOOD, RUSHED AT THE MAIN FORT.

effect of Isaac's attack and report to him. He now saw this boy running towards him.

The attack by the main body had been so fierce that it needed all the strength of the men in the fort to beat them off, and while the troops under Isaac had been seen in the beginning, yet their purpose was not fully known, and they were left to the attention of the side fort. Not until it was too late was the mistake discovered.

Three strong boys, with a huge beam of wood, rushed at the main fort near its point. They were too far away from the side fort to be very much hurt by its fire, and Isaac's men kept all their assailants well occupied.

Bang! bang! bang! the icy covering gave way—a hole; two or three more strokes of the ram and the wall would be down. A frozen ball struck one of the invaders in the head, and he fell as if shot.

"No matter, once more, lads, with all your might."

It was Isaac who took the vacant place. Crash! the wall gave way. One more stroke and it was down for some two or three feet. The boys dropped the beam and, taking their fallen comrade, retreated to a safe distance.

This breach in the wall was announced to Moses by his aid. He gave three long whistles with his fingers; in a moment, the five boys who had been concealed in the factory yard appeared on the wall at the back. They were overstocked with ammunition and fresh for the fight. They poured a raking cross-fire into the fort, and, under cover of this, Moses, with a detachment of men, re-enforced Isaac, and attacked the enemy's right once more.

In the fort the soft snow had given out, and solid balls of ice flew in the air. It was dangerous. It needed no command now to the invaders to return these deadly missiles. Wounded men were everywhere. Boys limped about the field or held their heads; some lay on the ground groaning. But the excitement was so intense that no one thought of pain or danger.

The terrific assault with frozen balls from the boys, high on the shed over the works, was doing deadly destruction—the walls of the fort were left unguarded. Moses sent his aid to Noel to tell him to make a united attack on the right, while he entered the breach in the wall with his men.

The invaders displayed new vigor. At the left entrance there was a hand to hand conflict going on. Joe Harris was rolling over and over in a terrible wrestling match with Tim Machin, while Doughty and Owen together were beating the front ranks back with great bravery.

The odds were now against the town-boys. One after another gave up to nurse the wounds made by the fire from the boys on the shed, and the attacking party drove their enemies back into the fort. At the same moment Moses entered the break in the walls made by the battering-ram. He sprang to the top and raised a white handkerchief. It was a signal of a victory and a truce; but so fierce was the contest that it was some time before the fighting could be stopped. There were so many wounded, however, that both armies were finally glad for a chance to rest.

The damage had been great. Moses had his cheek cut open; one of his eyes was quite closed and he was bruised in many places. One boy had broken his arm, while red spots on the snow, here and there, told of noses that had bled from the battle.

But the school-boys had won.

The next day, when school assembled, there were but two or three missing at the roll-call; but the class was like an army of veterans. Many limped painfully; bruises were on numerous faces, and great strips of plaster decorated the countenances of several boys.

The Master announced with a smile that no more snow ball fights must take place. The owner of the factory back of the wall, annoyed by the uproar, had the fort torn down that day and all chances of renewing the battle at Kings Common were done away with. But for many months were the doings of that campaign talked over.

" You ought to have been with us when we took the fort from the town-boys at Kings Common."

CHAPTER IX.

A SWIMMING MATCH.

Two years at school.

Moses had taken a mercantile course, and graduated with honors. The term had ended. When summer was over, he was to go into John-son's provision house, to learn business ways and fit himself for a tradesman or merchant.

He looked back on the days past with mingled pleasure and regret. Life at school, at first, had been nothing save sorrow; but now, at leaving, all was changed. He had many friends among those who had formerly scoffed at him. It was like tearing himself away from a battle-field, where he had won a victory. He had the feeling of satisfaction in his heart of having done something for himself and others—of having conquered a difficulty—and he was sad to leave the place.

To-day, the whole school, masters and scholars, were to go out into the country, along the Thames, where the boys might swim and play to their hearts' content. It had been the custom, for many years, to take this excursion before the final exercises at the closing of the term. It was a re-union—a chance for last words and the cementing of friendships for after life; it was looked forward to and talked over for many days beforehand.

The weather was sunny and warm. When they reached the farm-house at which they were to alight, the boys rushed madly through the fields, laughing, joking and playing all manner of tricks upon each other.

Horseham Meadow was a large open field, on one side of which was a wooded hill. The river ran near by, and the banks were shelving and gravelly—just the place for swimming. Half a mile up the stream was a public boat-house.

"Let's hire some boats and have a row," Hornby said to Moses. "Noel and I can take one boat, and you and Isaac the other. It would be a good thing to get some exercise before we go swimming; we can row back here and have fun with the boys who are swimming."

"I'll go if the others are in," Moses said. "But I don't know much about rowing."

They made their way up the stream. The banks were sweet with summer flowers. Startled frogs jumped from the grasses and plunged loudly into the water. The rattle of the kingfisher was heard as he darted swiftly from tree to tree or dived after his prey. Now and then, they came on lone fishermen, who grunted unintelligent replies when asked how many fish they had caught.

On reaching the boat-house, it was but a few minutes before the boys were in the boats and on their way down the river. Moses had never rowed before, and made his friends laugh by taking his seat with his face towards the bow. When they got off, he made many mistakes, and several times fell over backwards. It was some time before he could get in the way of the thing. Isaac had had very little experience—between them they made a very sorry exhibition. Noel and Hornby soon left them far behind. It was not long before they saw a third boat put out from the boat-house; when it drew near, the oarsmen proved to be Moses' old enemies, George Owen and Richard Doughty. These two rested on their oars. Both had lived in the country, and knew all about boats. They seemed to be in a reckless humor.

"You don't get on very fast," Dick Doughty said. "You fan the air too much. The blade of the oar is made to go into the water."

"They think they are in a flying machine," Owen sneered. "Some people think they do everything well, but they don't."

"Let them be," Moses said, as he saw that Isaac was about to fling some answer back. "What's the use. They are spoiling for a quarrel. Let's try it again."

So they rowed awkwardly down the stream. The new arrivals would not leave them, but went leisurely along, making all kinds of jeering remarks about their mistakes.

At last, the boats arrived at the bank where

the boys were bathing.   There were not many of
them in the water yet, and all wanted to be taken
out rowing.   Moses and Isaac took them off, two
at a trip, and gave them short rides across the
stream and back.

After a time, as they were about starting out,
and Moses was standing up with an oar in his
hand, he heard a cry and turning saw that
Owen and Doughty were rowing recklessly
towards him.   Moses called out a warning but they
either did not hear him, or did not care, for, in
another instant, there was a crash of the boats.
He tottered, tried in vain to keep his balance,
stuck the oar deep in the water without getting
any support, then dropped it and found himself
diving after it.   He came to the surface, almost
at once, and swam ashore, choking and blowing
the water from his mouth.   He was a sad picture,
dripping wet, and the boys, when they saw there
was no danger, roared at him.

"You did that on purpose, George Owen," he
said.   "I'll pay you out for it—see if I don't.
You've broken the boat, too."

"It's your own clumsiness.   You don't know
anything about boats; you oughtn't be allowed
to have one."

" We were standing still, and you ran into us. You are a coward; and I say you did it on purpose."

Moses was getting angry. But he found he must get his clothing dry before he was in a condition to discuss the matter.

" You had better take that boat back to the house, Isaac," he said. " Pay the man for the damage to it. That side is badly strained and it is not fit to use any more. I'll take off my clothes and dry them in the sun; you come back as soon as you can, and we will go in swimming."

The sun was very hot, but Moses knew that it would be a long time before his clothes would dry. However, he hung them on the bushes, near by, then went in swimming. He had learned the art in the large pool in the gymnasium at the school, had practised until he could sustain himself without fatigue, for a long time, and was a fast and vigorous over-arm swimmer.

It was a capital spot for the sport. There was a shelving beach of gravel, where the sun shone free, and a few hundred yards farther down, there was a steep rock, under the trees, and, beneath, a deep hole—a fine place for diving.

6

The water was somewhat cool, but Moses did not mind it; full of life and spirits, he swam among the boys and soon forgot his anger at the ducking he had received.

Even in the short races that they took while playing about, there were only two or three boys who were in any way his match. John Hornby was a much faster swimmer, but he puffed and sighed so, after his efforts, that Moses wished for a chance to test his endurance.

Presently, Dick Doughty and George Owen hauled up their boat on shore and came into the water. Without making any direct challenge, they tried to draw Moses into a race with them, but he paid no attention to their efforts. It was not long before Isaac Goldsmid and Noel Hilton came back from the boat-house. Moses went out to see them.

"It took all the cash we had to make it right with that boatman," Isaac said. "Those duffers who did the damage ought to pay for it."

"Never mind, let them be," Moses said. "It is not worth while fighting about it, with such fellows as that. We'll divide the loss. Come on in."

Soon they were all three racing up the stream.

Noel and Moses were evenly matched, but Isaac soon fell behind.

" Let's get Hornby and Joe Harris, and have a race up to that rock and back," Noel said, pointing to a rock up the stream, on the opposite side.

It was soon arranged and they made ready for a start. Doughty and Owen overheard the plans, and they also prepared to take part. Isaac acted as the starter.

"Are you ready," he cried.

"All ready," Noel answered.

" I will count one, two, three and go—then you start."

At the word they were off. There was no chance for any one to claim a foul; they all made so much noise in their struggles that it would not have been heard.

Hornby and Doughty forged far ahead, in the first few minutes; the other three were together. Moses' heart beat fast with excitement, but he remembered his experience, and kept up an even, careful stroke. It was to be a long race—at least half a mile in all. He felt confident that the leaders could not retain their advantage.

Half-way to the rock, that was fixed as the turning point, Joe Harris had fallen to the rear, while the others maintained their places. Then Moses began to slowly lessen the distance between himself and the leaders. George Owen held his own.

At the rock, the swimmers were so near together, that the boys who stood on the shore to watch them could not tell who was ahead.

Hornby was puffing and blowing like a grampus, and, despite his efforts, fell slowly behind; but Richard Doughty easily kept the slight advantage he had, and Moses and he crept slowly ahead of the others, with no variance in the distance between them. After a little, as Moses turned over, he looked backward and saw that Joe Harris had left the race entirely and swam ashore, and that Hornby was also disgusted and making his way to the other bank. Owen was still following, but the distance between him and the two boys was rapidly increasing, and he seemed to be laboring greatly. The victory lay between Moses and Doughty, and to the latter our hero now turned all his thoughts.

Doughty was one of those boys who are born wiry and strong. He did not trouble himself about exercise or regular hours, yet he had a physique that was the admiration of all who saw him. Now his endurance was being put to the test; so far, he stood it well. Moses was urging him on: every muscle the boy had—all the knacks he had caught in the art, were brought into play. The constant exercise in the gymnasium had hardened him—he was still swimming with a full, easy stroke. His brain was quiet now; he was determined to win. The old-time pluck that he had shown when he had stood the flogging, and when he had fought Owen, was once more at his heart.

They had covered more than half the distance from the rock to the starting point.

Moses had slowly drawn up on his adversary; they were swimming side by side, almost neck to neck.

Doughty was panting and laboring; he hurled himself onward with great over-hand strokes, the water surged about him wildly; but the training was beginning to tell. The months of work with dumb-bells and on the parallel bars, made the muscles of the boy at his side as hard as iron, and there was a calm strength in his stroke that had in it the look of victory.

The boys crowded the bank and began to cheer. The interest was intense, both swimmers felt new excitement and energy. Dougnty thrust himself ahead wildly, then, after a little time, fell behind again. A hundred yards or more and the race would be over. The fierce spirit of contest had aroused Moses' blood; there was no question of fatigue about him now. On and on with steady stroke. In another instant he would begin the wild race on the home-stretch, and he felt that he should win.

"Help! help!"—a smothered voice back of him.

He saw the boys on the shore crowd together and point over the water with anxious looks. He turned his eyes. No sign of Owen! Only some ripples over the quiet surface of the river.

In an instant Moses turned, and retraced his course with nervous strokes. All thought of the race vanished from his brain; in its place, he felt that strained, anxious horror that comes to every-one in the face of possible sudden death. He kept his eyes ahead, scanning the water for a sight of Owen. No sign; and he had certainly passed the point where the boy had gone down.

Then, as he turned over, he saw a sight, that all the sadness and suffering he witnessed in after years did not drive from his remembrance.

A body rose slowly to the surface, only a few feet away. The limbs moved, nervously, and the hands were clutching wildly for some support. Bubbles arose from the mouth, and the eyes, wide open, were set in the glare of despair. Death seemed looking from them.

Moses felt a chill at his heart, and, for a moment, could not move. But he recovered himself. He remembered the terrible stories he had read, where the drowning man clutched his savior in a mad grasp and dragged him to death. Fortunately Owen's head came near to him, ere he sank again, and Moses fixed one hand in the great shock of hair, then forced himself away, wildly, with the other. Owen struggled—his hands violently renewed their efforts to grasp his rescuer—but in vain.

The boys on the shore were so much interested in watching the course of events, that, at first, they did not have sense enough to put off in the boat that was drawn up near by; but when Moses cried loudly for help, so many of them rushed madly to the rescue, that it took some time to get the boat in the water and decide who should go in it.

Moses felt chilly; a strange stiffness shot

through his legs. Owen struggled, and several times almost succeeded, in grasping him; but the vice-like grip in his hair never loosened, and the pain of it probably aided Moses to hold him and keep him off.

But it could not last much longer. The boy felt in his heart that the end of all things was near at hand; a carelessness as to consequences came over him. His limbs refused to move, and he was chilled to the bone. He could not keep the grasping arms away. Suddenly they seized him, and he felt that he was sinking for miles below the surface. Then he heard Mr. Sever say:

" He will be all right now."

He was lying on the bank, in the hot sun, the teachers and boys about him.

" What became of Owen," he asked, feebly, after he had been rubbed and slapped with the palms of several hands until his skin was in a glow.

" He's all right, or will be in a little while. The boat saved you both."

A wagon was got from a neighboring farm-house, and the two boys were driven back to the coaching station together. There was not much conversation between them.

"Look here, old chap, I am sorry for the things I have done to you," Owen said, at last, just before they reached the station. " I'd been drowned if it hadn't been for you. There is not, another fellow would have done it."

He held out his hand, and Moses grasped it warmly.

He saw there were tears in his former adversary's eyes.

CHAPTER X.

AN EVENING AT HOME.

Amid all the trials of the world—the troubles at school, the unmerited punishments, the dislike of his fellow-scholars, and the strain of defeats, Moses had been comforted always by the sweetness of his home life. His mother and father were ever ready with the deepest love to help him, and Uncle Moses watched over his progress with a heart as kind as it was determined and just. So, too, Uncle Josh, on his visits, cheered the boy by his jolly ways, and lightened all his cares with the hopes and encouragements that he held out. Now, having conquered so many of the difficulties that beset him, and with these helping hands about him, Moses was almost happy. To be sure, there were little troubles, now and then, but with them a sense of freedom and power, and life was filled with more meaning to him.

At this time he was perhaps somewhat backward among girls, as boys are apt to be. He had not the shyness or false bashfulness that is often seen; but was very reserved, and found little to say. So, one day, when his sister Sarah told him she was going to give a party on her birthday, and that he must look his best and try to be jolly, she was greeted with a very wry face.

"Whom are you going to have?" he asked.

"Only a few. Bessie Johnson, Esther Goldsmid; your friend, Judith Cohen, and four or five others."

"What are you going to do, when you get them here?"

"Play games, and have something to eat. What more do you want?"

"Well, I'll be here, of course; but I don't care about it much."

"But you love *me*, don't you?" his mother said, smiling. She laid her hand against his cheek, and he leaned his head over on it. It felt soft and cool; his face was so warm by the fire.

"Girls I don't see the use of. They are *bothers* and they can't talk about anything."

" You are always the silent one, when they are about," Sarah said.

" I think all manly boys are," her father broke in, looking up from his book by the fire. He was a reserved man, but took a quiet, sweet interest in all his children, not the less deep that they had beside the double care of Rachel and Uncle Moses.

" But it would be so much better if they were not," Rachel said. " I want Moses to be natural and pleasant, manly in all things,"—she pressed the hand tightly that held her own.

" I saw Mr. Johnson to-day, and I have made arrangements for you to go into his store to learn business," Moses' father said. " They cannot bother you then, Moses. You can say you are too busy and haven't time to attend to them," laughing.

" Why don't you take me in with you, father? I'd much rather be in your store."

"I should spoil you," his father said, smiling. " You will get a better training outside, where you have some one to correct you."

" I wish you would let me go into the army. That's what I want most."

"Why there is no place for you there. We are forbidden everything, except trade."

"But look at Uncle Josh."

"He has special privileges, you know."

"Well, he says he can get them for me, too."

"I want you to learn business first. It will be time enough to talk of war hereafter."

Sarah and little Esther were filled with excitement on the evening of the birthday. Uncle Moses and Uncle Josh were among the guests, and none of the children enjoyed it more than the great soldier, with his laughter and jollity. In Blind-man's-buff, he rushed wildly to and fro, and when he seized a little girl, he was not content with kissing her, but put her on his shoulder, and carried her triumphantly about the room.

After supper when they were all gathered about the fire, and apples were roasting and nuts cracking in the ashes, the children insisted that he should tell them of a new game. "Something warlike," Esther said.

"My games would all be too rough for you," he said, "but you might have a play with soldiers in it."

They all wanted this, and were so persistent that at last Uncle Josh consented to help them.

With a bit of wire and two shawls, he arranged a stage for his drama. Moses, Judith Cohen, Uncle Moses and Rachel were to be actors.

There was much hurrying to and fro, on the part of Rachel, hunting costumes, and helping the two uncles to arrange the scenery. The audience was in a state of wild interest, long before the play began.

At last Uncle Josh commanded silence.

"This is a play without words," he said. "So I will explain the scenes as we go along. The first picture shows a young soldier called away to the wars. He is bidding his sweetheart good-bye."

He drew the curtains.

Moses was dressed in an old uniform of Uncle Josh, and such a tall fellow had he grown that it almost fitted him. He was holding out his arms to Judith, who stood near with her handkerchief to her eyes. Presently she looked up. How pretty she was in her childish innocence! A slight girlish figure, ruddy complexion, black hair and clear bright eyes. Moses threw his arms about her, and she sobbed bitterly on his gay uniform.

There was great laughter and applause on the

part of the audience; and they could not rest quiet until the actors were again ready.

"The next scene," said Uncle Josh, "shows his sweetheart at home with her mother. The post-man comes in with a letter and bad news."

Judith sat by a table, sewing, and Rachel opposite. The girl looked up, nervously, every now and then. There was a loud knock, that made them both start; and then a second, louder. Rachel went to the door. The postman came in —Uncle Moses. After much search he produced a letter. Judith opened it hastily, and then fell back in her chair, sobbing wildly.

"I must take part in the next scene," Uncle Josh said; "so you will have to see for yourselves what it is about."

When the curtain rose, the old soldier was seen, with sword in hand keeping off an army of foes impersonated by Uncle Moses, while he half carried Moses off the battle-field, seriously wounded.

In the final act, as before, Judith was seen at her work, but this time without Rachel. She was dressed in mourning. A knock came, and she went hastily to the door. A soldier entered limping with a crutch, and his arm in a sling.

She fell back, crying and frightened, and her lover, dropping his support, knelt at her side.

In the excitement of the play the crutch struck the candle on the table, and knocked it on the floor at Judith's feet. It was not extinguished in the fall, and in an instant, the flame had caught her light dress. Moses saw it, and with his hands beat out the fire before it could gain headway.

It all happened in a moment, but the audience were breathless, and the actors came forward, amidst a burst of applause that was very real and heartfelt, on the part of the older ones, at least, who knew the serious danger.

"I have ruined one of your best dresses, Sarah," Judith said, sorrowfully. "But you must be glad it did not burn it all up."

"I am gladder it did not burn you," Sarah said.

When the visitors had all gone, and the family was once more gathered about the fire, the moment before going to bed, Uncle Moses said:

"Well, Moses, do you still find girls a nuisance?"

His nephew blushed and laughed.

"Oh!" he said, "they are not so bad to play soldier with."

CHAPTER XI.

MOSES A CAPTAIN.

"I don't like tea and groceries as a steady business,"

Moses sat with Isaac Goldsmid in the latter's comfortable room, in his home at Morden.

"Why don't you come with us?" Isaac said. "Gold and precious stones are not as nice as the army, but you might like it better than where you are."

"Can I get a place, do you think?"

"Ask Uncle Moses; he has the say, you know. He says there is always a chance for good boys in our business," Isaac answered, laughing.

The friendship between the two had grown deeper as time went on. Isaac was becoming a shrewd, careful financier. He was, besides, vastly interested, not only in business questions, but in good works. The welfare of society was as much to him as personal wealth. His influence was always for the best.

"Don't go into the army," he said, when his friend spoke with him about it—and it was many times. "You can do more out of it than in it.

There is such great work to be done here; I cannot see much good in war."

Moses had begged, in vain, to be allowed to take up the trade of arms, but those about him were not willing to have it so. His father had articled him to a firm of which his neighbor Robert Johnson was the head, and Moses had faithfully served as an apprentice in the business. He still longed for the army; but certainly to be in his uncle's store with Isaac Goldsmid was better than his present position. Moses' uncle was a partner with Isaac's father in his business, and it was easily arranged that he should have a place with them, among the gold and jewels of one of the largest brokerage houses in London.

He had grown in the year since leaving school. He was nearly six feet in height, and by constant exercise had kept himself muscular and erect. He was a man in his stature and almost one in his thoughts. Happy by nature, his great flow of animal spirits, his lively conversation and gentle manners soon made him a great favorite with his new employers. The utmost confidence was reposed in him, and he was entrusted with the care of vast sums of money and bullion and precious stones.

There was one person about the office who did not like Moses, and Moses soon grew to have a feeling of distrust for him. This was Henry Bland, one of the clerks. He was hard-working and accurate in his ways; but, without any definite reason in his heart, Moses had that instinctive distrust of his sincerity, which so often exists without one being able to explain why.

The doubts that he held were one day much increased.

He was making a short cut through a side street, when he saw Bland coming out of a drinking-house, with two flashy men, who looked like professional gamblers or sharps. He spoke to him and passed on; but he was sure there was an agitated look on the clerk's face that showed that he felt he had been detected in suspicious company. Moses' doubts were greater when Bland came back to the office.

"Those were a couple of fellows I went with to see a sick man, who belongs to the same society as I do," Bland said, with a hard look of pretended innocence on his face.

The fact that he felt it necessary to offer such an excuse, without any one having accused him, was, of itself, enough to condemn him; but Moses, knowing him to be the only support of his mother, did not have the heart, on such bare suspicions, to speak to his uncle about the matter. The mere taking of a drink with two sporting men was not of itself enough to show him to be a bad clerk.

It was oftentimes necessary that large sums of gold and precious stones should be carried to other banking houses or customers, and it was Moses' duty to act as escort to the man that took the valuables. Bland was occasionally this messenger. With the jewels or money in a case or bag, he would walk ahead, while Moses followed, fully armed, on the lookout for sudden attacks. These trips were exciting, at first, and every corner seemed a hiding-place for a highwayman. But as time went on, Moses ceased his vigilance and the matter became quite commonplace.

Now that his suspicions as to Bland's steadiness were aroused, Moses watched him carefully, and in following him along the street was always ready for trouble. For a long time, however nothing came of it. Bland was more than ever attentive to all his duties; there was in no way the slightest cause for complaint.

It happened, one day, that a large purchase of diamonds had been made by a customer of the house. They were to be a gift to a foreign princess on her marriage, and were worth a fortune. It was arranged that Bland should carry the jewels, and that Moses and Isaac should go with him as escort. At the last moment, Isaac was detained, and, as the delivery was a matter of time, Moses and Bland started without him.

Their customer lived in another part of the town, and, by the busy streets, the way was long. A much shorter route could be taken by means of the back streets and alleys; into these Bland turned. Moses was about to remonstrate with him on the danger of these secluded ways, but his fears seemed foolish, and he said nothing. His personal bravery sometimes made him indifferent to risk. He kept a sharp lookout, however. In his coat pocket was a pistol, ready for action, and, in addition, he carried a heavy stick, loaded at the end with lead.

At the corner of a small street, crossing the one they were on, was a low, dingy dramshop. The upper windows were closed, and there was an air of darkness and dreariness about it, heightened by the fact that a light shone over the door leading into the bar. It was a house that, at night, Moses would have thought of in connection with murders, and hurried by; a house that, even in the daylight, struck him with a feeling of suspicion.

At the corner Bland paused. There was no one in sight.

"Shall we turn down this way?" he asked, nervously.

Moses thought it strange that he should put such a question; he knew Bland was familiar with every street about there, and must have known that their way lay directly ahead.

"Certainly not; go right on," Moses replied.

Then he heard the sound of the opening of a door, quietly, and before he could turn, his stick was wrenched from his grasp, his arms pinioned to his side, and he was struggling with some unknown enemy. A second assailant seized Bland, and was evidently trying to rob him of the jewelry.

The attack was so sudden, so unexpected, that Moses was taken by surprise. The grasp of the man who held him was like a band of steel. In vain he struggled to free himself. He strained every nerve and muscle in an effort to throw the fellow over his head, only to be met with a strength and weight that proved it useless to try

and rid himself in that way. Then he endeav-
ored to twist himself out of the vice-like grip.

A violent struggle followed. Over and across
the pavement, around and around they whirled.
Moses was mad to desperation when he saw that
Bland was on his back in the street, the second
robber going through his pockets. In a moment
more he would have the case containing the
diamonds.

Again the struggle with his assailant began.

Moses noticed that the cellar window of the
house projected into the street, somewhat, and
was without a grating. There was room enough
for a man's legs to go through. He forced the
robber backwards toward it. In the excitement,
his assailant did not suspect the object. He found
himself hurled against the side of the house;
then his foot slipped and he dropped down-
ward, letting go of Moses in the shock of his
descent.

Meanwhile, the second robber had taken the
case from Bland, and was making off with it.
Moses left his late assailant, and bounded after
him. He had always been a fleet runner, and
before the thief had crossed the street, he felt
someone throw his whole weight on him, and, in

an instant, he was struggling on the ground in the grasp of a man as strong as himself.

Moses now had a chance to use his weapon. He drew the pistol from his pocket, and using it as a billy, struck the man on the head. Ere he could raise it for a second time, the other robber, having climbed out of the window, again attacked him—this time with his own cane.

Moses fired his pistol, but in the excitement and struggle missed his aim. The man rushed at him and struck a fierce blow with the stick. For a moment, the three struggled furiously together. The odds were against Moses and he would certainly have suffered had not help arrived, the pistol-shot having attracted the attention of several persons.

In a few moments, the streets were as filled with people as before they had been empty. Both the robbers were captured and taken to the lock-up. Bland was nowhere to be seen. The diamonds were safe, but Moses suffered many weeks from the blow on the head he had received from the cane.

The robbers were afterwards convicted, and, in their testimony, Bland was shown to have been led by them into the crime.

But he had fled to parts unknown and was never caught.

It so happened that the customer who had purchased the diamonds was the Lord Lieutenant of Surrey County, and a great friend of Uncle Josh. So pleased was he with the bravery of the boy that he sent for him that he might thank him. When he learned of his military ambition, he questioned him as to his knowledge of tactics and the science of arms. Moses did not know the meaning of it all, at the time; but one day he received a letter with the official stamp of the government, which told him that his majesty had appointed him a lieutenant in the militia of Surrey County.

Moses' happiness was too great for expression. The trouble with Napoleon had begun, across the channel, and the militia was put on a war footing. There was incessant drilling, training and marching, but never too much for Moses. And those about him came to look upon him as one fit for a commander—kind, yet firm, with a thorough knowledge of every detail of his duties.

After a time, the captain of the company accepted a commission in the regular army, and Moses Montefiore was given his position. There was not one of his comrades, who did not feel in his heart that the most fit man had been chosen for the place.

How happy he was on parade. What a glorious life was open to him. His broad shoulders, his six feet of manhood, his clear, flashing eyes, made him admired by all, as he marched at the head of his men.

CHAPTER XII.

THE CHOICE OF A LIFE.

" Uncle, they have made me a captain in the militia. Don't you think I could get a commission in the regular army, now ?"

" You still wish to give up gold and precious stones for military glory ?"

" Do you think I can ever be fond of trade when there is a chance for the other ?"

" But you have been very successful. There is no better man in our house than yourself. I should not know what to do without you. You will grow wealthy if you keep at it."

" Oh ! but I don't care for that, so much ; I want the life of a soldier. Look at me, Uncle ! I can be proud of my strength without conceit, can

I not?" and he stretched his arms over his head, while his Uncle was silent in admiration.

He was fully six feet in height, with a heavy figure of perfect proportions; he held his head with that erectness that came from his long, self-imposed military training. His eyes were deep : there was a possession in their glance that forced his listeners to hear him. His features, in their clear outlines were as if cut from stone, and his ways, in all things, were those of a soldier. There was about the whole man that over-abundance of life and animal strength that made his uncle feel a thrill of pleasure in his heart when he thought of him, in the uniform of the guard, marching to battle. Surely God had made this boy to be a leader of men!

"I never can like the confinement of trade," Moses went on; "I want to be out in the open world. When I hear the sound of a trumpet or the tramp of troops, my heart beats, and I want to throw down the diamonds on the floor, spring over the counter and join the admiring crowd that follows after."

"But think of the hardships, the sufferings, and the difficulty of success to any one—more so or you, because of your race."

"Look at Uncle Josh, though. He is one of us, and, yet, he might have a 'Sir' to his name did he wish it so. I don't think of the toil; I am made for that," and he clutched his great muscular hand, nervously. "Besides, there is almost as much opposition against us in trade as in the army."

They were at the house of Asher Goldsmid, at Morden, having been invited to dine with a number of distinguished guests, among whom were Lord Nelson and Uncle Josh. Uncle Mocatta said no more, at the moment, for dinner was announced. He had not spoken seriously to Moses for some time on the subject of his ambition for arms. His nephew had worked faithfully, with great success, and he had trusted that years would remove the longings for military glory. But it seemed to have burned in his breast during all this time, and had now broken out, the more fierce that it had been so long confined.

At dinner, Lord Nelson and Uncle Josh had many military stories to talk over, and, finally, his uncle spoke of Moses and his wish to enter the army.

"If he is as fearless and indomitable as his

uncle, and as brave as he is big, I think we can do something for him," Lord Nelson said, glancing over at Moses.

A look of pain passed over Rachel's face, but her son did not see it; and, after dinner, over their coffee and cigars, he spoke to his Uncle Josh again about the matter.

"Could I get a commission in a regular corps, do you think?" he asked, anxiously. "There will be great wars soon, and I must be in the battles. I am of age now, and they have made me a captain in the militia, you know; but that is not exactly regular, and I will have no chance there."

"I am certain the king will grant my request, if I ask him to let you serve him. On my return from Africa, when I declined the honors he offered me, he told me that if he could ever do me a favor I might ask it. And his Lordship will say a word for you, no doubt."

Lord Nelson, after a time, spoke with Moses about his wish.

"It has always been my hope, since I can remember," the young man said. "It is in my heart; it will always be there. I am hardy and strong and I feel the force of will in me to compel

success in the army. I know I will succeed there,
if I am not killed."

The Admiral was impressed with the physical
beauty of the youth, and his fearless, earnest
ways. He felt, as he looked at him, that the
military instinct was there. "Soldier" was
written in the face and eyes.

"I will make it a personal matter," he said;
"and, coupled with your uncle's request, and your
position in the militia, it will certainly be easy
to arrange it. There are chances opening now
which may give you plenty of fighting and
glory."

Moses' heart was filled with wild exultation.
The longings of his life, it seemed, were all to
come true. He felt the blood bound in his veins.
He had that strange animal desire to use his
great strength upon something, that he might
show the joy that was in him. Away with gold
and jewels and ledgers, bonds and stocks and
loans! Out into the open field of battle, where
foes did not lurk, but were seen and known at
once! Life, free and untrammelled! Victory for
his country in her cause! Fame with her crown
of laurel!

That evening, in the library of his father's

house, at Kennington, Moses sat before the fire
with his arm over the back of his mother's chair.
His hand caressed her hair, and, now and then,
she would reach up her own small one to be held
in his firm grasp. Under the lamplight his
father was playing with Horatio and Sarah, while
Uncle Moses sat in a great easy chair, near by,
lost in thought.

The logs crackled merrily upon the hearth-
stone, and to Moses the sound was like the firing
of musketry, and he heard in his ears the blare
of trumpets; he dreamed of marching troops and
great battles, where he won honor and glory and
came home with decorations on his breast—and
his mother kissed his hand.

"Do you wish so much to leave me?" she
asked, softly.

"Mother, some of us are born for one thing,
some for another, and when the longing is in our
hearts, it seems best for us not to beat against it.
You know how much I love you, don't you?"

"You have been the best boy in the whole
world," she said, gladly yet sorrowfully; "but I
want you to stay with me. It is not death that
I fear for you; but you could do so much more
with your life in other ways."

" What way, mother?"

"Since the time of the first legend of our race, mankind have asked themselves the same question: 'Why are we placed here on earth? why must we suffer? to what end is it all?' To every one the question comes sooner or later. To evade the answer is to herd with the brutes; to answer it only according to the fierce desires of the body, or the longings of the mind, it is but little better; only to him who gives to it his heart and soul can be known even a part of the truth."

" But, mother, I have always loved the soldier's life. I am made big and strong that I may stand its hardships; and you see I have conquered the feeling against me, so that they have made me a captain in the militia. Lord Nelson and Uncle Josh will both help me to get a commission in the regular army. Why can I not work out my life in that way?"

"I do not say you cannot; but I ask you, my dear boy, to take the reason of life to your heart. How can your own best be lived—as a soldier with arms and war, or as one who battles for a truth?"

"But what am I to do? Is it to be grind-grind-grind, all the years, to lay by money—or a life of fire and action and freedom?"

Uncle Moses, who had been quietly listening to the discussion, now spoke.

"Moses," he said, "you know how much interest I take in our race. The books that I have written have shown you some of it, but more than all those, you know it from my teachings to you. I have watched over you from the day of your birth; you know the concern I have had in your studies and my love for you. I have seen your progress with a heart of joy—if you were my own son, I could not care more for you."

"I can never thank you enough," Moses murmured.

"I have hoped to see in you one who might take up the work of your people, and help to free them from the bonds thrown about them by tyranny and persecution."

"Oh! if you could only see the way," Rachel said, clasping Moses' hand tightly in both of her own.

"Our nation," Uncle Moses continued, "is the greatest of the world. It has seen the Pharaohs pass away and the Empires of Assyria, of Babylon, of Persia, of Macedonia, and of Rome fade into nothing. Greek art, philosophy, legislation and civilization have risen and fallen in a short period

"OH! IF YOU COULD ONLY SEE THE WAY," RACHEL SAID.

of its life. The Ptolemys and Cæsars were mere passing shadows beside it; nations and sects that have persecuted us are long gone and forgotten. To-day we pursue our traditions unchanged, with faith and hope in our hearts, in the belief that the light will come at last. We have been the teachers of the world for thousands of years, in spite of persecution; yet, with all our efforts, we are trodden down, now, by the powerful, all over the earth, because we only believe a part of their faith."

"What could I do?" Moses said, thoughtfully.

"I will buy you a position in the Board of Brokers; the number of our race which can be admitted there is only twelve, but I can arrange a place for you. If you will work, with your abilities and opportunities, you can make a fortune and then devote your life to your fellow-men. What soldier's life can be as great as that of the man who marches forth to battle for the good of his race and of mankind; to fight oppression and persecution and suffering; and, in the place of triumphal arches, to raise schools and colleges?"

"I fear I should not be able to accomplish all that!"

"But the motive of your life," his mother said, softly. "Think of what I told you. Live up to the best in your heart."

"Our people have made the world nobler and better in all its history," Uncle Moses went on. "Our faith is the corner-stone of the Christian religion; the laws, the philosophy, the poetry of our books, have left an influence on all mankind and taught them the unity of God, purity of human life, and charity to everyone—and yet we are despised. They have put upon us the bonds of slavery; they persecute us when we try to break them, and, after taking away our rights, condemn us, because we do not become great. There is work here for all of us. The task is before you, Moses. Use your life to help your fellow-men, to rescue your race and make the name of Jew known over the world for what he is—the most intelligent, industrious and faithful of all men."

"I know, but I think I am meant for a soldier, somehow."

"War, as you mean it, at the best, is cruel," said the soft voice of her whom Moses loved so well. "Many things must be done at command that make my heart sick to think of. Whether he believes in his country's cause or not, the soldier must fight the same. Battles may be unavoidable, they may be glorious; those who fight them may be good and faithful and pure!— but oh! the sorrow, the sufferings they bring. If you can only see your life so, it must be that you leave us; but will you, for the sake of those who love you, who honor you, think well before you choose?"

"You know I will, mother."

" You have for your motto a very old and homely saying in our family : 'Think and Thank.' Be thoughtful and kind ; be courteous, and, for your star, keep the walls of the Holy City before your eyes."

"But there have been kind and thoughtful soldiers, whose battles were fought for the welfare of all the generations after them."

"That is true; all I ask of you is thought; to choose the best way to live your life. It will always be a comfort to you to be doing the best you can, in the best way you can. There is one safeguard for us all. Remember, that no one can . ever detach himself from his relation to others. His influence will be felt, not alone in the present, but upon the future destiny of the world. The

responsibility of our lives is in their help or hin-
drance to those about us—those who come after us."

His mother put her arms about his neck and
kissed him, and he clasped her close to his heart.

Were his dreams to pass away for ever? Must
he give up the glory of arms? Should the troops
march by, on their way to strange lands, to see
strange peoples and fight the battles of his
king, and he not be there? Must he crush out
the wild longing that beat at his heart, to go into
the world and, by the strength that was in him,
conquer and subdue the enemies of his country?

Sitting so, in the dim light, no one ever knew
the struggle that passed over him, between the
love for the glorious life he had planned and
that set out for him by the stern fates.

In the silence that followed his mother's words,
he listened to a drum, afar off in the streets of the
town. It grew fainter and fainter, and, at last, as
he strained his ears to catch the dying sounds, he
found that what he heard was only the ticking
of the clock on the wall. His mother's fair face
looked up at him, and he felt her kisses, soft
and warm, and gazed into her eyes, deep and
true, and filled with a great love for him.

The fire died away, and only embers glowed

on the hearth; the rattle of musketry in his ears ceased, and no army went by, with banners and music—the dream of fame passed away with the smoke of the logs that he watched with thoughtful eyes.

And then Moses made his choice.

CHAPTER XIII.

THE END OF A DAY.

An old man sat in an easy chair, on the lawn of his country-place, and his eyes looked out to the setting sun.

Spring and Summer had flown away, and Winter was at hand; when the morrow dawned a hundred years would have passed over his whitened head. He did not notice the autumn flowers, the changing colors of the trees or the waving grass in the meadow. Down in the woods the squirrels and rabbits played as merrily as in days when he had wandered here, his heart full of youth's ambitions, and wild longings to be a soldier and fight the battles of his king.

He fell to musing. While the warm October air whispered to him, he found himself lingering with faltering footsteps over the pathway of his life.

Though so many days had gone by, what was his reward?

He was no statesman, holding in his hand the welfare of nations, nor a poet, bearing a wreath of laurels; he wore no gaudy uniform, nor were there any ranks of armed men ready to obey his word of command; he could not recall the rattle of musketry or the roar of cannon amid conquests on bloody fields of battle—the dreams of his youth, as he had dreamed them, had not come true.

Yet he lived over again perilous adventures by land and sea; in strange countries and amid strange people he stood, once more, before governors, cardinals, ambassadors, kings or emperors, to wring from them the rights of his race; he suffered, amid scenes of sorrow that almost broke his heart, and marched, without arms or army, in the enemy's country, amid storms and dangers, to the rescue of his down-trodden brethren. Even in his heart, grown placid with the weight of so many years, these memories of his life stirred up the spirit of old that had called him to the field of war.

He had worked for his race with a pride in the glory of their achievements that had made princes bend to him; he had thought, loved and acted according to the faith of his forefathers, the truth and the law; he had done good in all the ways that life offered to him, and thousands whom he had freed from persecution, lifted up their voices in prayer to him, while colleges and hospitals that he had erected were monuments to many busy years of toil.

He felt the touch of the sword which had knighted him for work done in the cause of humanity; and upon his forehead rested the crown of good deeds.

And then he knew it was no dream, for in his hands were messages from many lands and peoples of the world, that told him of the reverence he had won—not from his own race alone, but from those who, in the days of his youth, had counted all men of his nation as enemies.

The times were changed since then.

Those who had been forbidden to follow any but the limited pathways of trade, now were set at liberty to achieve success on such broad avenues as they might please; then, they were slaves, to be beaten to earth and condemned because they did not climb the heights of fame; now they were free among men to work out their destinies, according to the truth that was in their hearts.

Moses Montefiore was glad and murmured a prayer and thanksgiving that God had been gracious to him and granted him power to do good to those who suffered and were oppressed; and he saw how small must have been his conquests under the banner of arms, compared to the victories for his race that had been given into his hands, as a soldier in a greater cause.

The sun set in a mass of cloud, gleaming with a thousand rays of crimson and purple and gold, and a bright light shone over the world; there fell a great peace upon the old man's heart, as he watched the radiance of the day pass away; and he saw that night was at hand, and he was weary and dreamed he heard his mother's voice calling him, and he longed only to lie down and rest.

www.ingramcontent.com/pod-product-compliance
Lightning Source LLC
Chambersburg PA
CBHW020408030726
47496CB00007B/2368